SECRETS RETURN

Leftover Girl Book 2

C.C. Bolick

SECRETS RETURN

FROM THE AUTHOR

.

If you are reading this book, hopefully it's because you enjoyed *Leftover Girl,* or at least found yourself wanting to continue the story of Jes Delaney. If you haven't read *Leftover Girl,* please consider diving into that book first. While I try to relate previous events as much as possible, I hate to weigh the story down with what's already happened, especially when there's so much fun stuff to come.

I'm thankful to everyone who has read *Leftover Girl* and I enjoy all of the interaction with readers. When I wrote this book, I always planned for it to be a series, but I wasn't sure if anyone beyond my circle of friends and family would want to read more (and I wasn't always sure about them). I decided to release the book and see what happened. To my surprise, people started buying it, for which I am grateful.

As people who know me will say, I don't write to get rich. Writing is the way I deal with stress from my job. Creating stories makes me happy. I have no expectations of ever quitting the day job (which I find rewarding despite the stress). The only thing I'd like to know is if people connect with and enjoy my stories. After reading this book, please consider leaving an honest review on Amazon and/or Goodreads.

Please visit my website www.ccbolick.com and leave feedback anytime. I'd love to hear what you've got to say. The third book in this series should be ready in May of 2017.

I sincerely hope you enjoy reading *Secrets Return* as much as I enjoyed writing it.

C.C. Bolick

For Mazie,

Because she always believed

And I loved her dearly

CHAPTER ONE

Stuck

I stared at my bedroom door. One thought plagued my mind, same as it had every day for the last five months. Focus, I had to focus. I closed my eyes and wrapped my mind around the doorknob, imagining my fingers on the curved metal, turning until a click sounded and the door slid open.

Opening my eyes, I sighed and sank lower in the bed. The door hadn't moved.

A gentle tapping sounded against the door and I jumped. "Rachelle called again," Mom said from the other side.

"I don't want to talk to anyone."

"Jes, you need to get out of this room."

Straightening against the headboard, I closed the book in my hands and shoved it under my pillow. My mind had drifted often in the months since Chase left, but I wasn't successful at finding my power then either. I was tired of waiting for him to return with the proof he promised, the secrets of my past I already knew to be true. Maybe not all of it, but I remembered standing on the platform as if it happened only the night before. Tears still bit at my eyes as I pictured his head sinking below the dark water.

I took a breath, forcing my voice to a safer place. "Wednesday was the last day of school. There's no reason to leave my room now."

"Your friends are having a party at the lake. Rachelle has called eight times in the last two days."

"I have no friends." I looked out the window. Clouds were boiling with the summer heat, threatening a hundred degrees of misery for our Alabama town, although a full week remained in May. Credence had to be one of the hottest places I'd ever called home.

"Jessica Delaney," Mom said as she opened the door. "You will get out of that bed and quit moping about."

"What does it matter? Who cares if I spend the entire summer in bed?"

"I care." She sat on the edge of my bed and I tensed as she took my hand.

"You have to care about me. Isn't that like the first commandment of being a mom?"

"It's more than that, Jes. Your father and I are worried you've become, well, disconnected. From school, from friends, from us. You remembering was never important enough to cut off the world."

Me remembering was everything. It was how I'd make things right with Chase. I pictured his face that last night at the mall, after insisting I wasn't the girl he'd been searching for. I'd screamed for him to leave, but his pain felt like a knife in my own back.

If only I could tell someone. "Dad said the doctors

would help me, but no one can help me. I'm just as broken as when we came to Credence. Maybe if we'd stayed in Atlanta…"

"Don't say that." She pulled my head to hers. "You grew so much over those first months, and when you figured out the truth about the Naples, I couldn't have been prouder of the way you reacted."

"You should have told me the truth." After five months, the betrayal I felt from their lies still burned as it had on my birthday. No, Jessica Naples' birthday. Mom and Dad adopted me at five; I'd always known. But they didn't have to lie and say the Naples were my real parents. For eleven years, I thought those people abandoned me, and now I knew they didn't hang around because I wasn't their real daughter. No one but them seemed to know what happened to the real Jessica Naples.

Mom pushed a loose strand of hair behind my ear. "Learning the truth on your own made it real."

"Yeah, that's what Dad keeps saying." But I didn't learn it on my own. Chase showed me the truth, made it real. Yes, I'd finally remembered the night I lost him all those years ago, but if he hadn't told me, the spaceship in my head would have been dismissed as a dream. I wouldn't know we were from another planet or that I'd been lost in New York, not a 'four-year-old runaway' as the papers said.

"You should call Rachelle," Mom said.

How could I get out of going to the party? Maybe my old fear would save me this time, since it always seemed to work against me before. "You'd really drop me off next to a huge body of water? After the way Dad freaked out when he found me at Angel's party last fall?"

Angel's place had been close enough to the river for her backyard to include a dock.

She pulled away. "Are you still afraid of water?"

Lie, I told myself. But seeing the concern in Mom's eyes, I couldn't. "No."

"Then I'll take you to the party. Rachelle has been a good friend these last few months."

Strange how much could change in five months. Now my parents acted as if I'd never been afraid of water, when last fall they acted as if my trip to the little creek in the woods behind our house with Bailey was worse than the day I skipped school. I looked at my hands as guilt clashed with rage. "Rachelle is not the friend I need."

"I know," Mom said, patting my hand. "Bailey should be back sometime this summer."

Should? Like she and Pade should have come back for spring break? Yes, my best friend who hadn't bothered to pick up the phone in more than a month. Bailey was Mom's niece and had been the best friend I'd always wanted, until she left to live with her dad in Colorado. Pade had gone too—but his departure gnawed at my heart in a different way. I'd turned down his offer to stay for me. I pictured his eyes, filled with hurt after my words, but I could never tell Mom about my feelings for Pade. Not when he was her nephew.

Mom had no idea I wasn't worried about Bailey. Jealous maybe, but I worried about Chase. I shuddered to think where he might be or who might be keeping him from returning.

Mom leaned closer. "I know how you must feel."

I smiled at the ridiculous words. No way could she ever understand.

* * * * *

Later that night, after my annoying twin brothers went to bed, I tiptoed down the hall and into the bathroom. Gently, I clicked the lock and flipped on the light above the mirror. Staring at my brown eyes, I took out both contacts, dropping each into an empty spot in the holder.

From my pocket, I pulled out the pair of glasses Chase gave me as a birthday gift. The blue-gray metal gleamed in my hands as I raised the pink lenses over my nose. Since the gift was our secret, I'd made sure no one ever saw me wearing the glasses. Behind the lenses were blue eyes.

The same blue eyes as my brother. If only I could see Chase again.

I grabbed the thickest towel from the shelf above the toilet and spread the plush beige along the bottom of the tub like a blanket. Climbing in the tub, I stretched out my legs and opened the book in my hands. Removing the green bookmark, I settled with an arm to each side of the tub and leaned my head back.

It was going to be a long night.

* * * * *

Lake Credence teased us through the trees along the paved trail. The entire lake covered more than twenty acres, according to Mom, and ran alongside the road in several spots. We passed a campground and two pavilions before topping the hill leading down to the lake's sandy beach area. Mom pulled up near the bathhouse but didn't turn off the van.

"Got everything?" she asked as I climbed out. "Your sunscreen?"

"Put some on this morning," I said and grabbed my bag.

"With all this sun, you'll need another coat." Mom stared at me but didn't shift the van into gear. "Are you okay?"

I thought of Pade, always asking the same annoying question, and smiled. "No, but if you'd feel better staying, you're welcome to spend the day embarrassing me in front of all my friends."

Smiling at the mention of friends, she slid on her sunglasses. "What happened to that daughter of mine who used to worry so much about what everyone else thought?"

"Jes," Rachelle called from across the parking lot.

"Rachelle's mom is bringing you home, right?" Mom asked.

We'd only had this discussion ten times. "Yes."

"Be careful," she said. Her window rose before Rachelle reached my side. The van circled around the parked cars and disappeared down the stone drive.

"I thought you bailed on me again." Rachelle pointed to my bag. "You better have a swimsuit in there."

"Mom took me shopping last night."

"About time you got out. Come on, you can change in the bathhouse."

Inside the bathhouse, I pulled on the swimsuit, a one-piece mixture of blues and greens. Rachelle, in a bikini that hugged every curve, stood just outside the curtain. What would she think of the skirt that hid my hips completely? If only she knew I'd never owned a bathing suit before last night.

"Oh no," I said, rummaging through my bag.

"What is it?" she asked.

My heart beat fast, almost too fast as I pushed aside the curtain and poured the bag out on the counter between two sinks.

"Girl, you're freaking me out."

"I forgot my sunscreen."

Rachelle laughed. "Is that all?" She pulled a can from her bag. "You can use some of mine."

I read the label and cringed—SPF 15. The mixture was like water compared to the tube Dad always gave me, but it would have to be enough. I sprayed every inch from my ears to my feet and then started the stream again.

"Easy," she said. "I didn't say you could use it all."

"I might need it all," I said, but she only laughed again.

I drew a breath when I saw the water, dazzled by a thousand tiny sun rays. The lake spread to the edge of sight, fading as it reached the sky.

"Waterfall," Rachelle said as she followed my gaze.

Dozens of our classmates took turns diving from two boards on a high-rise platform halfway across the lake. Others tossed a volleyball over a net that stretched across the sandy beach. The only person missing was Tosh, not counting the three people I thought of every time I opened my eyes in the morning. I waded into the water behind Rachelle, but never felt an ounce of fear. Chase would most definitely have been freaking out.

For one afternoon, I waded through the laughter and fun, talking to everyone from Credence High who cared to open their mouth. After those first tense minutes, I didn't think about the sunscreen. I didn't think about the secrets no one surrounding me could know. I didn't think about Chase, or Bailey, or even Pade, and thankfully no one mentioned their names. It was like being in Arkansas, at the farmhouse before Dad got sick. Before we had to rush to Atlanta. For years we moved, north in the summer and south in the winter, each time getting closer… to Alabama. Mom's perfect hometown.

I looked around for Rachelle, spotting her under a tree far from the beach, knees hugged against her chest. Her head rested on her knees.

"Hey." I lowered to the ground and crossed my legs beside her.

"Now isn't the best time," she said.

I froze, stunned by the cruelty in her voice. "What's wrong?"

We sat in silence. Her body shook next to me, barely at first and then in all-out spasms. I put an arm around her shoulders but she jerked away.

"I told you…" she said, but the words dissolved into a sob. Rachelle leaned into my embrace.

People laughed around us. The volleyball bounced at our feet and a girl ran by chasing it, never looking down. Rachelle moaned half-words and apologies, but she wasn't making anything up to me. I doubt if she knew I was there.

"You shouldn't like me," she finally said. "I wouldn't be my friend."

"Tell me what's wrong," I said, cringing at how much I sounded like my parents.

She threw her phone at the sand. "I hurt someone."

"We've all done that."

"No," she said. "I've hurt someone and I can't take it back."

"Angel?"

Rachelle beat her palm against her head. "Angel is stuck on Skip. This is worse."

"Someone from school?"

"Someone I met at the bowling alley, right after Christmas. We talked online every day. I never told you about her."

My stomach churned. "Can't you apologize?"

"My friend… she killed herself last night. I… I just heard."

"Oh my god," I whispered and pulled away. "What happened?"

"She… I can't talk about it. She wouldn't want me to say."

Her tears fell again, this time not as full-body sobs, but as a gentle stream of pain that would never cease. I pulled her head to my chest, hugging her as the moisture fell on my arms and legs.

The sun drifted closer to the trees. People faded from the beach and the water became a sheet of glass.

She wiped her nose with her arm. "Have you ever thought of… you know…"

"Killing myself?" I stared at the bathhouse. Skip Greene laughed as he and Angel walked up the hill to the parking lot, neither noticing our lonely tree. "The night after Lisa died, I almost tried."

Rachelle gripped my arm. "Are you serious?"

"I took one of Mom's kitchen knives and held it to my wrist."

"And?"

"I couldn't do it. I kept thinking of Mom's face

when she found me."

"I never imagined you…" She sighed. "I'm glad you didn't do it."

"Yeah," I said with a small laugh, "me too."

"Did you ever think about it again?"

"Never. After that night, I was glad I didn't go through with it." I thought of Chase, of our day at the lake when I learned of his power. Our birthday. "The next day was one of the best I can remember."

"When I first read the message, I thought about it. But my mom has planned a trip to Washington D.C. this week. We're going to see my real mother, and there's so much I've got to say to her first."

"Then wait a week before you decide," I said. "Think about it for seven days. Dad's taking us to the aquarium on Saturday, but we'll talk on Sunday. Just you and me, all day."

"Promise?" she asked weakly.

"I'm not saying it's okay to kill yourself, because it's not. But I'm not going to sit here and act like I never thought of it myself. Promise me you won't do anything crazy before Sunday."

Rachelle nodded and rose to her feet. "I'm sure Mom's waiting in the parking lot."

The car ride home felt longer than any trip I'd made with my parents in our crisscross of moves. It wasn't what Rachelle had said that bothered me, or what I admitted to almost doing. Rolling my window down, I took a deep breath as the air fanned my cheeks.

"Jes," Rachelle said, "Mom's got the air on."

"I'm sorry," I said. "It's just so hot in here.

Rachelle and her mom laughed. "It's not hot in here," Rachelle said, handing me her compact. "It's just you. You're sunburned."

I stared at my face in the tiny mirror. Mom and Dad were going to kill me.

* * * * *

"Jes," Mom called from the kitchen, "is that you?"

"Yeah," I said, but slipped past the doorway and ran to the upstairs bathroom. I locked the door and flipped on the light. My reflection in the mirror was enough to make me want to skip dinner. Heat radiated from my skin along the deep red patches covering my face and arms, and streaked from where my bathing suit ended to my feet. Pale marks on my shoulders traced the straps of my bathing suit.

"Jessica," Mom called from the other side of the door.

I held both of my cheeks as I struggled to breathe. My teeth began to chatter. What was happening to me?

"Are you okay in there?" Mom asked, her voice rising with concern.

"Mom," I whispered.

The door handle shook. "Open the door," she said.

I turned the lock and she flung open the door. Mom stared, not speaking, not moving, not breathing.

"I'm sorry," I said. "I forgot my sunscreen." The old 'I'm in trouble' sick feeling settled in my stomach.

Mom reached forward and took my face in her hands. "Oh, honey."

I lowered my head and the tears fell. "I'm sorry."

"How do you feel?" Her words swam in my head. "Are you sick?"

I felt like my insides were coming apart. "I don't

think so."

"You've never been sunburned before. We've always been so careful."

"Do you think Dad will be really mad?"

"Is that what you're worried about?"

"Yeah." I took a deep breath. "I know I probably can't get sick like Dad did, even though he always makes me wear that oozy sunscreen. Rachelle's mom said not to worry because I couldn't have inherited any kind of cancer gene from him since I'm adopted."

"Jes…" Mom said.

"It's okay."

She hugged me close. "Do you feel like eating dinner?"

"Maybe later."

"How about you lay down for a bit?" She helped me into the bed and pulled the comforter over me as if I were five years old again, sobbing over a nightmare. "A bad sunburn is nothing to take lightly. Please tell me at the first sign of sickness."

"Don't worry, I'll be fine."

She kissed my forehead and stood back. Her eyes lingered on the angry red skin not hidden by the green comforter. My face. My arms. Mom's face creased with more than her usual lines of worry. Something was really wrong.

My stomach churned again.

* * * * *

Bad dreams returned that night and followed for the next five. Every nightmare started with Chase leaving and ended with me waking in a sweat, which wasn't caused by the blisters on my skin. I watched a hooded figure follow Chase around corners and down dark alleys. When the figure turned, revealing amber eyes, I screamed Chase's name and reached for his arm, but he never noticed me running behind him. Each time I opened my eyes, I found it impossible to shake the feeling Chase was in trouble. But where was he?

I crept down to breakfast on Saturday morning, feeling sicker than any moment in my entire life.

"How are you feeling?" Dad asked, glancing over me.

I lowered into the seat across from him. "Okay." The blisters had begun to disappear and the redness in my face had faded. I should have felt better, but I didn't.

"No sickness?" he asked.

"No sickness," I said. "The cream Mom brought me is helping." How could I tell them about the sun making Chase sick? I tried to think of all the scientific explanations he'd used. Did I have a chance at convincing them? *Mom, Dad—I'm from another planet. The radiation from Earth's sun is too much for my alien body to handle.*

When he turned to the twins, I closed my eyes. If only I could silence the ringing in my ears.

"Perhaps we should cancel the trip," Dad said.

"No," Danny and Collin begged.

"Boys," he said, "if Jes is sick then we should stay home. We can go to the aquarium when she feels better."

"I'm fine." I opened my eyes. "I didn't sleep good last night."

Dad leaned back in his chair, eyes fixed on me. "You would tell me if something were wrong?"

"Of course," I said.

Mom took one of his hands. "Justin, she's sixteen. She knows the difference between right and wrong. If Jessica says she's okay," she said, looking my way, "then we should believe her."

Everyone held their breath as I stood. Mom's eyes willed me to tell the truth, and Dad's begged me to show their trust was well founded. The twins only cared about getting to the aquarium.

Despite my dizziness, I managed a smile. "Let me get dressed and I'll be ready."

* * * * *

I crossed my legs and lifted one knee high enough to hide the book in my lap. It was tough to get comfortable in the small space of the van. "Yeah," I said, though I wasn't sure what I'd been asked.

Someone grabbed my leg and yanked, forcing me to drop the book between the seats.

"Mom," Danny said, "Jes is reading again."

I looked up to see the boys snicker. Collin snatched up the book and waved it in the air.

"Jes," Mom said. "I told you no more books. All you've done for the last three months is hang out in your room and read."

"When did reading become a sin?" I mumbled.

Mom turned around. "When you decided to read instead of live."

"Everything in moderation," Dad said, from the driver's seat. "Too much of anything is bad."

"Fine." I crossed my arms. Instead of watching the boys laugh in triumph, I stared at cars rushing by. More lanes had formed and lighted signs appeared above the next exit. Atlanta was close.

I closed my eyes. The aquarium was starting to top my list of worst ideas ever. If only those stupid boys hadn't insisted.

Dad had always promised the boys a visit to the aquarium, but never managed to find the time when we lived in Atlanta. Maybe it was because of his cancer treatments or maybe it was my fear of water. Either way, the boys begged him for more than a year.

The walk across the parking lot wasn't as bad as I feared. By the time we got to the first exhibit, however, I was out of breath. Walking to the edge of a huge tank, I pressed my hands against the glass and stared into the wall of liquid blue before me.

"Does the water bother you?" Dad asked.

"Not at all," I said, forcing a smile.

"Maybe this trip *was* a good idea," Dad said. "You needed to get back to the world."

As he walked away, the first impossible wave of dizziness hit. The room spun as I gasped for air. People gathered to my left and right blurred. The ringing in my ears returned, this time shooting through my head and converging behind my eyes. Benches called to me from beyond the stingray exhibit, but the crowd of people forced me to hesitate. Could I make it through without falling? I had to find a place where I could think without the noise. Then I spotted the stairs.

A dozen or more stairs led to another level above. I thought of Chase as I climbed the stairs, about the time a wave of nausea rolled over me. Grabbing a side rail, I clung to the metal. Below, people crowded the glass in front of the sharks. As Danny touched the glass, I closed my eyes, praying for the dizziness to stop. Where were my parents? I had to tell them.

"Mom," I called, sure she'd never hear my whimper.

"Jes?" Mom was shoving through the crowd in the direction of the stairs. "Honey, are you okay?" she yelled.

"I'm fine," I mumbled, but felt better knowing she was near.

"Jessica!" Her shout was muffled in my head. I heard the worry, and I felt instant guilt. All I could think about was how she must have felt when Dad was sick. I needed to be strong.

Mom screamed for Dad as I released the rails. She would have to see me standing on my own to be convinced, and in some strange way I thought I might be okay with her there. The ringing increased until I no longer heard her voice, only watched her lips move as she ran for me. Her feet pounded in slow motion. Her arms reached for me, distorting at the edge of sight.

I clamped both hands over my ears, but the noise only increased. My legs gave way and I fell down the stairs, sliding across the rough edges until my back landed on the floor. I stared at the ceiling, a sea of white with strokes of color swimming before my eyes. Someone grabbed my hand. Lips moved, calling my name. Asking what happened with alarm. Horror.

An envelope of darkness surrounded me as my mind shut out the world. Fear faded with the voices to merely a laughable nagging at the back of my brain, reminding me of how I once made light of the fact they'd never love me. Couldn't love me, for I wasn't their daughter.

I didn't want to be alone.

At least the ringing had stopped.

CHAPTER TWO

Comatose

My head felt as if a bomb had exploded within the walls of my skull. The bed beneath me bounced and skirted from side-to-side. I stopped. I moved. I stopped again. Lights above glowed beyond my eyelids, but I couldn't force my eyes open.

I felt weaker than that winter in Texas when I had the flu, puking up every drop of water I'd managed to choke down for three days. Mom had held me when I rolled to one side of the bed and hung my head over the plastic tub she'd brought.

This was worse, scarier even than when Dad was sick. I couldn't understand the voices but I knew at least one belonged to Dad. The smell of sterilization brought to mind the long halls and white coats I'd come to expect with visits to Dad. We were at the hospital in Atlanta.

Voices whirled around me, with words I couldn't understand. Someone was crying. No, I was alone. I tried to force my eyes open to a darkness that held me like a cocoon, but devoid of any warmth. If only I was back home in bed, wrapped in my green comforter. The air chilled the skin on my face. Someone kissed my forehead.

No, I was alone again.

The beeping remained, a constant reminder I was broken. I thought of how the phone had beeped the night after Lisa died. One steady sound, always in my ears no matter who came to my bedside, no matter who begged me to return from… I wasn't sure.

I wasn't even sure if I cared anymore.

* * * * *

From my hiding spot behind a chair with black and green plaids, I heard the woman speaking like all the times before, but this time I understood her words.

"Will you really leave if I choose not to go?" Desperation filled her voice, but also a sort of pleading. Somewhere between the two ran a line of defiance. She would stay regardless of his choice.

Inching around the chair, I could see only the man's back before a window that stretched to the ceiling. He stood as a statue, head lowered.

"It's better if you stay," he said.

"Am I getting through to you?" she asked.

He sighed. "I could stop the attack."

As she came into view, her head shook. "When you are discovered, your children will pay the price."

"My family is important, but I cannot allow innocent lives to be destroyed. I should not have trusted…" His head dropped into his hands. "When I leave, the others will understand and accept you in a role

I could never fill."

She moved to his side and lowered her head to match his. "I may hate you for placing them in danger, but I cannot blame you for choosing honor. You think this makes you a failure?" Her voice softened and I strained to hear. "You are so much more to all of us than you can see."

When she looked up, the room was empty. "You were so much more to me." Wiping her tears, she opened the door with a wave of her hand. Her shoes clicked along the hall.

If only she'd noticed me in my dark corner. I wanted to follow her, but more than that I wanted to follow him. Yes, I'd follow him to the ship. Maybe stop him.

That was why I followed him. He never kidnapped me. My father had no idea I ran behind him, desperate to make our family whole again. Surely he would have stopped me if he knew.

Memories flowed as if a valve had shifted to wide open. Instead of small bursts, the old dreams weaved together in one smooth flow—the long hall, the ship, the platform. I'd climb aboard to make sure he wasn't alone.

But then I'd be alone.

Chase. Where was Chase?

Closing my eyes, I pictured Chase in the alley. Except for his hair, he looked the same as he had on our last night in Credence, when he accused me of leaving him. The white-blond now almost reached his shoulders. The same hooded figure from my dreams followed close, but I couldn't see a face.

The alley faded and I stood on the metal platform.

Chase reached for my hand, pleaded with his eyes for me to save him. The hooded figure grabbed him, trapping him in the blanket. The amber eyes glared at me before pulling him into the water.

Chase took a final breath before his face disappeared, followed by his fingers.

A man gripped me tight, struggling to keep us from falling as he sped down the long hall.

I blinked and I stood in an open room, with another man staring down at me.

"Van, don't do this," my father said.

The man with evil eyes lifted the gun and pointed it at me. He laughed. "If she's so important, this bullet will surely find a way around her."

"No!" My father leapt forward.

Strong arms gripped me as a single bullet exploded. The sound hummed with the sheer power of a bolt of lightning in my ears. My skin prickled as the arms forced me to the floor.

"Justin," a woman screamed.

I opened my eyes as light exploded within every inch of my vision. Somewhere a beep sounded, the low and steady beacon that promised safety or at least reality. The air still reeked of industrial bleach. A hand gripped one of mine.

"Please, Jes," Dad begged, "come back to us."

"Dad," I whispered, but the word sounded like a stranger's voice in my ears.

"Oh god, Jes." Dad pulled my hand to his cheek.

I flexed my fingers against the rough hair and his hand relaxed. Although my neck felt like it had been fused to the bed, I managed to turn just enough to see Mom take my other hand.

"Honey," she said, "I'm so glad you're back."

"Mom." I tried to squeeze her hand, but my energy was fading fast. "What happened?"

"You've been in a coma," she said.

Dad released my hand and rubbed the tears from his eyes. "How are you feeling?"

If only I could nod. "Okay," I managed, but my head felt like I'd been spinning on a tilt-a-whirl.

"You were screaming," Dad said. "We rushed into the room."

I closed my eyes, focusing on my last dream, as if by will alone I'd force the memories back. "He was drowning."

Mom's hand tightened around mine. "Who was drowning?"

"Someone… I knew."

Dad leaned over me. "What was his name?"

"I don't know." I closed my eyes. Was I still dreaming?

"You were saying a name." Dad took my hand again, almost fighting against Mom. "You screamed it over and over."

Our eyes met as I willed the fog in my brain to clear. "Who?"

He sighed and released my hand. "Chase."

* * * * *

A machine beeped to my left. I opened my eyes to darkness except for a gentle glow on the far wall. Someone had left the TV on for me?

I stared at the flat screen as the characters came into focus. It had been many years since I watched Mickey

Mouse, so long the characters didn't look the same. Donald argued, waving his arms in the air, but I couldn't hear his squeaky voice.

A pain seized my abdomen. Grabbing the rails, I craned my neck to make out the bathroom door. Swinging my legs over the side of the bed, I heaved, already out of breath. Slowly, I lowered my feet to the floor, easing my weight from the bed. Drawing myself up, I doubled over as my insides clenched and I felt sure my stomach would split, spilling my guts across the floor.

The feeling will pass, I told myself and took a long stride toward the bathroom door. My legs gave out and I reached ahead as the floor rose to meet me. The tube along my arm nearly sucked the needle from the back of my hand. My face struck the tile, a solid sheet of ice against my cheek.

The cold spread through my body as I lay there, bitter about remembering that night again and nothing more, filled with hatred for the world around me. I steadied my shaking hands and tried to push up, but my arms collapsed beneath the weight of my body.

I angled my head to see the clock. Squinting, I tried to make out the numbers, but couldn't since my contacts were out. It would have to be enough to watch the hand crawl as it made a full circle. Thirty seconds. A minute. Feet pounded along the hall as someone screamed, "Doctor, stat!" but the sound grew and then faded beyond the beeps. The beeps were steady, though not quite in rhythm with the clock.

Just when I feared the off-beat sounds would drive me insane, voices approached the door.

"She's going to be okay," Collin said.

"What if she…" Danny's voice faded to barely audible.

"Dad was here for months, and he didn't die."

Their feet shuffled past the door and down the hall. A few minutes later, five to be exact, I heard their voices again.

"We should go in," Collin said.

"I can't see her like that," Danny said.

"She might be awake."

"I can't see her like that," Danny repeated, his voice giving way to tears.

Through all the years we'd been a family, I'd never heard Danny make a sound that I felt in the pit of my stomach. He threw a fit once and cried in the electronics section of a store when Mom refused to buy him a video game. He'd cried about every friend he had to leave after each of our moves. Even when Dad was sick and Mom prepared us for the worst days of chemo, he never cried in a way that convinced me he thought of someone beyond how the drama affected him. Tears welled in my eyes.

Their voices faded again.

I laughed at myself, stuck on the hospital floor. Mom had often worried about how nasty our kitchen floor was, even though she mopped it daily. Once when I was a child, she'd sent me to my room just for crawling across the floor to watch her cook.

Seven minutes later, their voices chimed again, this time stopping outside the door. I sighed, not getting my hopes up. The door creaked, slowly at first, and then banged against the wall.

"Jes!" Danny yelped as he raced to my side.

"We'll help you up," Collin said, grabbing my arm.

The twins managed to pull me up to sit before them.

"We'll get you back in bed," Danny said.

"Bathroom first," I said, my voice a rotten mix of pain killers and dry hospital air.

"What are you doing on the floor?" Collin asked as he and Danny again tugged on my arms.

In their eyes flashed all the fear and worry from their voices in the hall. They were the only ones who'd never looked at me as if I were damaged. I'd always been the strong one for them. A tear slid down my cheek.

"Don't cry," Danny whispered.

Collin put an arm around my neck. "We're sorry about making you go to the aquarium."

"And the book," Danny said. "We're sorry about the book."

"What's going on?" Dad asked from the doorway. He pushed the boys back and lifted me to the bed.

"I was trying to get to the bathroom," I said as the tears flowed.

"I've got this," Mom said, rushing forward. She took my other arm. Between her and Dad, I made it to the bathroom.

Humiliation burned in my cheeks. "I can go by myself."

Mom's voice was steady. "Why should you have to when I'm here?"

"I'm sixteen."

"Which means I'm the mother of a sixteen-year-old. You're never getting out of my sight again."

Great, I thought. Now I'd never find a way to search for Chase.

* * * * *

The beeping came again—my beeping, not Dad's as it had been during those months in Atlanta. Someone took my arm and lightly tugged a piece of tape, adjusting the IV line. The nurse began to hum, a country song I think, and pressed some buttons. The beeping stopped, before restarting in the same rhythm.

I considered begging her to turn it off, but I didn't have the strength.

I kept my eyes closed, hoping the nurse would leave without asking any questions. It was too early for explanations, or late I wasn't sure, and I didn't want to see the needle in my hand. If I looked at the tube, at the machine connected to me, I'd have to accept the fact I was stuck in a hospital bed. All those months I dreaded the elevator ride and the clean smell that tickled my nose, and now it was all for me.

She tugged on a can of sanitizer that hung near the door and rubbed her hands together. I laid frozen in the bed as she shuffled out of the room.

A voice spoke low and I focused on the source—a TV in the next room. Someone screamed the letter 'C.' "Sorry, no C," a man said. Someone called out three words and the male voice rose. The clapping and music that followed caused my head to ache.

In my mind, it seemed so simple. Touch the button along the TV's edge and the picture would disappear, with the sound. I pictured the button, imagined pressing it with my finger.

"Nurse, my TV!" a man yelled.

The door to my room closed with a gentle click. Someone was nearby.

I opened my eyes as a terrible thought gripped me. "Rachelle!"

"She isn't here," said a voice near the window. Pade turned and light slipping through the blinds formed stripes across his chest.

Struggling to sit, I pulled myself up with the rails, but my legs refused to move. My IV line caught on one of the rails, again nearly ripping the needle from my hand. The pain was intense, but even more so was the sense of dread at being chained to the beeping machine—if only the needle *were* ripped out of my hand. "You don't understand."

Pade rushed to my side and took my arm, unwinding the tube. "No, I don't, but you need to relax. Just lay back and tell me."

"Rachelle," I said, close to tears. "Is she…"

"She was here yesterday, but you were sleeping. Her parents drove her up to see you."

I sighed. "Thank goodness. I thought she…"

"Rachelle is fine. Now you, on the other hand, had everyone flipping out."

My eyes darted around the room. "Where am I?"

He took a long glance around the room. His eyes stopped on the machine next to my bed. Why did he hesitate? "You're in a hospital," he finally said. "Didn't your parents tell you?"

I remembered lying on the floor. I'd guessed we were in Atlanta but never asked. Had they told me that first day? No, they'd been more focused on asking about Chase. Great, now they knew I wasn't okay with him leaving. They'd probably hire me a shrink. "I don't think we got that far." I shook my head. "That means we're in Atlanta. That means you're—"

"Back." Pulling a chair close to the bed, Pade took my hand in his. "You've been in a coma."

Still darker than midnight, his hair now reached beyond his ears. I found myself smiling at the longer hair. If only I could touch it. "For how long?"

"Forty-one days."

"*What?*" That meant it was July. I'd lost a month and a half?

"Everyone was worried. I was afraid you wouldn't wake up—I've never been so afraid."

I squeezed his hand, feeling the raw pain and fear in his voice flow through me. "I'm sorry."

He did a double take. "Jes, you're not going to lie in a hospital bed and apologize for being in a coma. This time I won't let you."

"Did they tell you how I got sick?"

"Sun-poisoning. My mom could explain it better; she knows all the medical terms."

Of course, Aunt Charlie was a nurse. Shifting the pillows around my head, I rolled onto my side. "I can't believe you're here. You guys never came to the hospital when Dad was sick."

"Mom did. You just never saw her."

I smiled weakly. "I bet my parents have been freaking out."

"Everyone has been freaking out."

I pulled my hand away. "Are you going back to Colorado?"

Pade smiled, this time with a warmth that reminded me of the Pade I'd grown to love. He reclaimed my hand. "Just try and get rid of me."

* * * * *

"You gave us all quite the scare," Dr. Baynor said from a chair next to my bed.

I watched as the nurse entered my vitals on a tablet. "What happened to me?"

He leaned back and crossed his legs, holding one knee with his hands. "You were in a coma."

It had been nearly a year since I'd seen Dr. Baynor. How ironic that Dad's main doctor would also treat me. "Was it cancer, like what made Dad sick?"

"Of course not, honey," Mom said. She and Dad sat holding hands on the plastic couch beneath the window.

Dr. Baynor smiled. "Not exactly, but we think it might be kind of your dad's fault." He looked to Dad. "All those years he made you wear the sunscreen left you with minimal exposure to the sun's radiation. Getting so much at one time caused your system to go into overload."

Because, like Chase, I couldn't handle the sun. If only I could tell them without getting a personal invitation to the psych ward.

"This overload forced your system to shut down. I won't bore you with technical terms, but I will say I've never seen a case quite like this."

Yeah, I'd bet on that.

"As it turns out, Justin and several other cancer survivors underwent some serious testing last fall."

"In Tokyo?" I asked.

Dr. Baynor nodded. "The results of these skin tests helped us formulate new drugs to help future patients fight their cancers faster."

"So, then I did have cancer?" I asked. "Did you give me radiation?"

Dad cringed. "Don't say that word."

Dr. Baynor chuckled. "My, you are intuitive. No, we don't consider your sickness cancer." He rubbed his chin. "I've heard of rare cases where people developed an allergy to sunlight. I'm not sure if that's what happened here, but strangely enough the new drugs seemed to help heal your skin faster. We kept your room like a dungeon for more than three weeks, and it was still a few more before you woke up."

"Am I banned from going outside now?"

"Jessica," Dr. Baynor said, his voice serious. "You need to be extremely careful. I've made light of some of our discussion to keep you at ease, but it's no small miracle that you're alive."

His words washed over me. I felt real fear of ever going in the sun again. But the drugs—somehow they'd made me healthy again. If only Chase knew of this discovery. If only… I slammed a palm against my forehead. I'd probably never see Chase again.

"What's wrong?" Dad asked.

I pulled the sheet up close to my face. "All of this… it's just more than I can handle right now."

Mom stood. "She needs rest."

Dr. Baynor shook his head. "Lorraine, your daughter's had a year of rest."

"How did you know?" I asked.

"What?" Dr. Baynor asked, turning back to me.

I looked at Dad. "How did you know you'd get cancer?"

He frowned. "What are you asking?"

"All of those years we wore sunscreen, even before your cancer and that tub of goo you started making me wear every day. How did you know?"

Dad lowered his head.

"Justin's father died of the same cancer," Mom said.

Stunned, I pulled myself up. "Why haven't you told me?"

"I didn't want you to know last year." Dad put an arm around her neck. "He refused the treatments, as if what they had back then was all that great. Why do you think I've signed up for test after test? At least something good came out of me being away." He looked up, meeting my eyes. "I'm sorry this happened to you."

Pain and love shined in his eyes, dueling with the guilt. I knew what happened to me wasn't his fault. But how could I ever tell him?

* * * * *

I uncovered the tray, inhaling as the smell of rosemary chicken breast wafted up. My stomach begged for the wonderful aroma, but I wouldn't get my hopes up this time. After two weeks of breakfast, lunch, and dinner at the hospital—not counting the burger Bailey hid in her purse, I was starving for some real food.

"Don't worry," a voice said beyond my door.

Climbing from the bed, I peeked around the half-open door to see Pade on his cell.

"I know you are," Pade said, while rubbing his eyes. "No, don't leave. I'll be back in Credence tonight." He ended the call as Rachelle came around the corner.

"What's going on?" she asked.

He shook his head. "Nothing you can help with."

Rachelle put her hands on her hips. "You didn't answer my question."

"Are you going to see Jes?"

"If she's awake this time."

Pade turned and I ducked back behind the door. "They just brought her dinner."

"Are you going in?" she asked.

"No, I've got to get back to Credence. Tosh needs my help."

Rachelle laughed, her typical brand of disbelief wrapped with irony. "Can you really trust anything Tosh says?"

"Maybe not, but I've got to go. Please, don't tell Jes."

"I won't," she said. "But you should."

When his steps started down the hall, I jumped back in the bed and pulled the tray table over my lap. I ripped open the plastic fork and knife, stabbing the chicken, but the tip of the knife merely broke off and landed in the mashed potatoes. I hung my head as tears burned in my eyes.

A searing pain shot through my chest, straight to my heart. Yes, I'd sent Pade away. But right or wrong, he'd come back. And now, he was leaving to see her. Would Tosh always come between us?

"Hey."

I glanced up from the chicken and threw the plastic knife at the far wall in disgust. Rachelle stood in the doorway.

"You can come in," I said. "It's safe now."

She tiptoed to the foot of my bed and looked around, her eyes shifting from the chair full of my clothes to the couch weighed down with bags of books the boys had brought as a peace offering.

I pointed to the chair, trying to focus my attention away from Pade. "Don't worry about the clothes. Sit on them or move them—I don't care."

"I'm not staying." She took another look around.

"How are you?" I asked, staring at the girl who'd tried to be one of the best friends I'd ever known. She couldn't help the fact I wouldn't let her in.

Rachelle swallowed and formed a stiff smile as she stared back. "I should ask you the same."

"Getting better every day."

Her smile never faltered. "Yeah, me too."

Beeps sounded in the next room. Nurses rushed by my door, shouting to a doctor down the hall. The beeps became a shrill alarm.

She peered through the doorway. "Is it like this every day?"

"No," I said, "just on Fridays."

Turning back to me, Rachelle managed a laugh. "Don't ever come to a party without sunscreen again."

"I doubt I'll be going to any parties, especially those requiring sunscreen."

She swallowed again and looked at her feet. "Did you tell anyone about my… friend?"

"No."

"Good." She met my eyes for a quick second and walked to the door. Before stepping into the hall, she spun around. "Don't ever tell anyone." With those words, her feet barreled down the hall.

I leaned back against the pillows, wondering what just happened.

CHAPTER THREE

The Painful Truth

The Atlanta air was hotter than I remembered, or maybe it was the fact I'd spent most of the summer in a hospital room that wasn't much warmer than our fridge. The van was also quieter than I remembered. Mom and Dad stared ahead and the boys played games with headphones in their ears.

We pulled up in the driveway almost two hours later. Luckily, I'd slept for half of that. I smiled to myself, wondering if I was going to turn into Rip Van Winkle and sleep my life away.

Nothing much had changed in the foyer or the kitchen, except for the pile of mail spread across the table. The sink was empty and the dish drainer held not a single fork. Even the red mixer with its silver bowl sat in the same corner of granite as if never used. I wondered when Mom had last cooked a meal in our kitchen. I looked around the living room, taking in the lack of pictures on the walls and thought of Chase. I burst into tears.

"Tell us what's wrong," Dad said.

"You'd never understand," I yelled and ran up the stairs. The boys stared from their doorway as I passed, but I didn't look at them. Stepping into my room, I slammed the door behind me and leaned against the wall. I lowered myself to the floor, hugging my knees to my chest as the tears fell. They'd never understand who I was or where I'd come from.

My eyes grew heavy with all the tears and my mind drifted.

"Jessica," a voice whispered.

I opened my eyes to Mom, who was seated across from me, leaning against the bed. She stared as I reached for the door. It was still closed.

"You fell asleep," she said, as if reading my mind.

"How did you get in here?"

Mom sighed. "Through the door, of course, but I closed it so we wouldn't have an audience." She pointed at the wall separating my room from the boys.

I wiped the moisture from my eyes. "I'm tired."

"You were in a coma for almost two months."

"I never meant to get sick."

Her voice was calm, with a level of control I'd never noticed. "Before the coma you weren't well for a long time."

I lowered my head in my hands.

"Jessica," she said, her voice rising, "we can't help you if you won't tell us what's wrong."

The seriousness in her voice made my skin crawl. "Nothing."

"Something is bothering you."

I rubbed my hand across the back of my neck. "I don't want to talk about it."

"Honey, we *need* to talk about it."

I took a deep breath. "I've been depressed ever since Chase left, and then Bailey—"

"Bailey's back now."

Smiling in agony, I wanted like crazy to tell Mom the truth about my dreams. Would she believe me? "When I was in the coma…"

"Yes?" she asked.

My nervous sigh echoed through the room. "I dreamed constantly." The memories were still a fog, so I closed my eyes. "My real parents were there. Someone tried to kill me. I heard a woman screaming…" My eyes flew open. "It was your voice. You were screaming Dad's name."

"What exactly did you hear?"

"You screamed 'Justin'."

Mom moved to my side and took my hand. "When you awoke from the coma, you were doing quite a bit of screaming yourself. I ran into the hall and called for your dad several times before he rushed into the room."

The dream had felt so real and yet… it wouldn't be the first time I mixed the before and after in my dreams of the past.

"Dr. Baynor said people in comas report all sorts of strange experiences. Would you like to talk about it?"

I looked away. "Talk about what? Apparently that dream wasn't really of the past."

"Are you okay?"

So, we'd made a full circle. I stood in disgust and jumped onto my bed, tugging the comforter over my head.

Mom didn't move from her spot on the floor. "Maybe we pushed you too hard. Maybe we should have stayed at the hospital another week."

"No," I shouted. "I'm not going back there. It was bad enough when Dad was in the hospital. Now I just want my life back."

"Are you sure?"

I'd never been more sure about anything. "I had some issues in school and I missed Bailey like crazy. If everything will go back to normal, I'll be fine."

"School starts next week, but you don't have to rush. We won't make you go back until you're ready."

I laughed bitterly. "What if I'm never ready?"

"I've already arranged to home-school you for a while."

"Mom, I'm fine."

She stood. "Want to help with dinner?"

Finally, a normal question. I threw back the comforter. "Sure."

Mom stepped back, eyes wide. "We're having pizza. You really want to help?"

"I just did three weeks of physical therapy with only hospital food for breakfast, lunch, and dinner. What do you think?"

She grinned and reached a hand out for mine.

* * * * *

That night I sat at a picnic table Dad had added to our backyard. I pressed in my earbuds and listened to all of the music Bailey had downloaded for me over the summer. "Don't want you to miss anything," she said, but I still resented her for not staying in my room long enough to talk about why she'd never called. Some best friend she turned out to be. Staring at the sky, I wondered which star belonged to Chase, while hating myself for not remembering precisely which one he'd pointed out.

I focused on the music player, only inches from my fingertips, and wrapped my mind around the plastic. *Move across the table*, I thought and closed my eyes. When I looked again, the blue screen was more than a foot away. Excitement flooded through me. Had I really moved it?

When Dad sat down beside me, I jumped and pulled out the earbuds.

"Don't get uncomfortable," he said, holding up his hands. "What were you doing just now?"

I looked up. "Counting the stars. We used to do that, remember?"

"Of course," Dad said, "back when you still cared about learning the constellations. Now what do you think when you look at the stars?"

"I'm wondering how many of those stars have planets and how many of those planets might be someone's home."

Dad chuckled. "Probably most of them."

I couldn't see if the smile also danced in his eyes. "You believe in life out there?"

"Maybe not what we're used to, but it's kind of lonely to think we're it." He put a hand over mine. "What shall we do tomorrow?"

There was only one thing I wanted to do. "Can we go to the creek?"

"The one you got in so much trouble over last year?"

I nodded.

He pulled back his hand. "Tell you what—we'll go

there tomorrow, but not until after dark. We'll have a midnight picnic. Your mom is going to love this."

"Dad?" I asked.

"What is it?"

"What if you hadn't found me in New York?"

Dad hesitated. "I would've found you. Lorraine always says it was fate, right?"

"But what if you didn't?"

"You shouldn't worry so much and you shouldn't try so hard to remember. I promised to help you, but you've only moved farther from us. That wasn't my intention."

"I've tried, Dad, really I have. I don't think it's possible anymore."

He put an arm around my shoulders. "You'll remember when you're ready."

"I was ready last fall."

He squeezed. "All you've remembered is a name and a date. Are you sure there isn't more?"

There was a whole lot more, just not what I needed most. I needed time to figure out what happened that night. What could be so bad I wouldn't want to remember?

"There's more, I can feel it," he said.

"I had a memory last fall, when you were in Tokyo. My real father," I started, but choked on the words.

"Yes?" he asked, his voice sharp.

"He was holding me on his lap, reading a book. He called me Kay Ray." And I had called him Daddy.

"Did you see his face?"

Dad's voice felt wrong. Had I said too much and upset him? I never wanted him to think I'd trade all the years we had. Again, I tried to make out his eyes. "No."

"Sometimes I think your mom and I had it wrong." He sighed. "Would your life be better if you'd never heard of the Naples?"

I laughed. "And tell me what instead?"

"At five we could've told you anything. Maybe even that your mom and I were your real parents."

I considered keeping my current name forever, and the thrill of knowing I'd been loved by two people unconditionally. Two people who I'd built real memories with, who were right in front of me. "I'd be okay as Jessica Delaney, if you and Mom hadn't told me different." There was some truth in my words. I could feel my love for them both, rising up to merge with the pain of losing the life I'd once had.

"That would have been a lie," he said, rising. "You'd be just as heartbroken learning the truth."

* * * * *

Bailey handed me another book as a hair dryer roared to life behind us. I flipped through the thick, glossy pages, each containing a different style of hair.

"I like this one," she said, forcing a page in my face. "Layers would look good on you."

"Take your time," Mom said, from the seat to my other side. "Make sure it feels right."

I glanced around the salon. There were two cuts, one perm, and a blow-dry session going on. Reaching across Bailey, I grabbed a mirror from the table beside her. Nothing had changed with the ragged brown falling from my head, or the inch and a half of white blond glowing like someone had painted my scalp and held it under a black light.

"Change will be good," Mom said as she flipped through a copy of *People* magazine.

Each picture seemed the same to me. Boring. Until I stopped on a girl with short sandy hair that spiked from her head.

"This," I said.

"*Yeah*," Bailey said.

The blood drained from Mom's face. "Don't cut it. Style it any way you want, but please dye it back brown like mine."

"But you said…"

"I know what I said, but after the last few months I'm not ready for this kind of change. Please, I want my daughter back. I want your hair to be brown like mine. Call me biased, superficial, or even a bad mom, I don't care." Tears formed in her eyes. "I want the daughter I love to look like me again."

I stared at Mom. She was none of those things. I loved her and would do anything to make her happy. "I'll keep it brown."

She wiped her eyes and smiled. "Really? All it takes is me begging?"

"No," I said, smiling back. "All it takes is you loving me. You've never said you wanted me to look like you. I always dyed my hair because *I* wanted to look like you."

Mom threw her arms around me.

Bailey snickered. "You're not going to cry again, are you?"

I wiped my eyes. "No."

She laughed. "I was asking Aunt Rainey."

Mom pulled back and grinned. "I hope we have a thousand more days like this."

* * * * *

My hair wasn't the exact shade of Mom's, but it was close enough. Her face sagged after our two hours in the salon, and I figured she'd take us home. To my surprise, she took us to an expensive restaurant downtown.

Mom chatted about new stores added to the downtown area over the summer, about classes starting, and anything else she could think of. When she spotted our principal, Dr. Greene, through the window, she went to meet him on the sidewalk.

"I love it," Bailey said.

"My hair?" I asked.

"Being back."

I stared at her. "You don't sound convincing."

"Bullship."

I choked on my tea. "What?"

"You can't imagine what it was like out there. In Colorado. It was ducked up."

Did I hear correctly? "This is getting weird. Are you cussing or what?"

"Dad wouldn't let us cuss. Pade and I made up all kinds of weird sayings. We'd change the first or last letter. Now I can't get the stupid games we played out of my head."

"You should have called," I said.

She lowered her eyes. "I'm sorry. Dad was so strict. He took our cell phones away in April."

Was she lying? "That's your excuse? Don't I deserve more?"

"Yes," Bailey said, looking at me again. "He didn't have a phone in the house, other than his cell. At eight o'clock every night we were allowed to call Mom. But I should have found a way."

"Why did he take your phones?"

She took a long sip of tea. "You know Pade always cussed more than he should."

"So did you," I said with sarcasm. "Before."

She nodded. "Dad didn't like it. He banned all cuss words from the house. One night in April, he and Pade had it out. Pade was determined to find a way to come home, and so was I. Mom didn't want to hear us complain about Dad. She wouldn't bring us back."

Bailey sighed and rubbed her arms. "We were eating that night and Pade let loose. Dad called him a screw-up and Pade told him off. Dad slapped Pade and my brother fought back. I was scared, Jes—they were throwing punches and… well, let's just say they gave it everything they had. Dad grabbed Pade's arm and dragged him to the library."

I pictured Mr. Sanders. He and Pade had stood level with the same dark hair. I'd seen him once, from across the yard on the night before Pade and Bailey left Credence.

"When I say dragged, I mean all-out kicking and screaming from Pade. Dad locked the door to his library, so I couldn't do anything but pound on the door and beg for him to stop."

My eyes grew as I thought of Pade. No one had ever fought him.

"I've never heard Pade use such awful words, but after a few minutes the room went silent." She swallowed. "When they came out, Dad wouldn't look at me. Pade was holding his jaw. My brother was crying, can you believe that? Pade ran for the stairs, but he's never told me what happened in there. Whenever I ask, he locks up and stares off into space."

"That's the only time they argued?"

"They argued almost every night—that was just the last time Pade raised his voice to Dad. Heck, it was the last time he even looked at Dad."

I stared at Mom, still talking to Dr. Greene outside the door.

"Sometimes I'd watch," she said. "Sometimes I'd hide in my room."

"What did Aunt Charlie say?"

"I didn't call Mom. I spent the next two weeks in my room. Literally."

"What about school?"

"We didn't go to school. Dad hired private tutors for math, history, and then some. It seemed like every day someone different showed up. When I wasn't taking those stupid lessons or eating dinner, I stayed in my room."

And I thought my past was messed up. "Was he in some kind of cult?"

"I'm not sure about a cult. He never talked religion or brought any weird preachers to the house. We didn't talk unless spoken to—that was usually reserved for dinner."

"Why all the black clothes?" I asked, pointing to her shirt. "Even your lips are black."

"It was to piss him off. Pade thought of it. We went through all the clothes he put in our closets and wore only the black stuff. Once a week, we went into town and were allowed to shop for two hours."

"I can't believe he let you buy black lipstick."

"He didn't," she whispered. "I stole it."

I shivered thinking about my one experience with

shoplifting. Lisa had convinced me to skip school. We'd rode to the Save-All where she gave me a quick course in stuffing my pockets and dodging the cameras. I didn't know it was all planned by Tosh, or that Lisa would leave me there to get busted for skipping school. An hour later she and Jarrod had died when the semi slammed into their side.

"I know it was wrong," Bailey said. "I slipped the makeup in my pocket and asked the cashier to ring up an extra pair of socks that was the same price. I never went back to get the socks."

"So, your dad was rich and you were stealing?"

"Yeah." She laughed. "That about sums up my experience in Colorado."

* * * * *

The moon that night was almost as bright as the sun. White beads of light glistened along the water's surface, giving the creek an ethereal feel. Sweat formed along my brow, for the August heat had not yet lifted for the night. I sat on the bank and removed my shoes, easing my feet into the chilly water. My toes slid along the rocks. Something grazed my ankle—maybe a fish.

Pade sat beside me. "Feeling better?"

"Sure," I said, staring across the water.

"You don't sound sure."

We sat in silence until he spoke again. "Don't take this the wrong way, but I'm glad you got sick."

"Thanks," I said.

"No." He turned to me. "I'm glad we had a reason to come back from Colorado. I thought Dad would never let us leave."

"Bailey told me how controlling he was."

"Oh yeah?" His shoulders sagged, mirroring the way I felt.

I shouldn't have asked to visit the creek, not when this was where Chase chose to tell me all about his home planet. My home planet. The smell of pine trees in the thick air almost choked me as the memories felt like something I could touch. "Have you talked to Terrance?"

If Pade noticed the waver in my voice, he didn't mention it. "I haven't been much of a friend for the past six months. I called him after coming back to Credence, but he hasn't bothered to dial my number."

"What about school? This will be your senior year—time to plan for college."

"Dad wants Bailey and me to start work in his business the day after graduation."

I was almost out of things to say. "What about football?"

Pade stared across the water. "I won't be playing football this year."

The desolation in his voice brought tears to my eyes. I turned away so he couldn't see my face.

"Dad made me promise," he said. "It's the only way he agreed I could finish school in Credence."

"Why does he hate football?"

"He's afraid I'll get hurt. He doesn't want me wasting my future on some 'stupid sport'."

"Bailey talked like he was some freak in a cult."

"You don't understand how rich he is. I always knew he had money, but all those years I had no idea."

"Bailey said he hired tutors and wouldn't let you go to school."

"His house is more like a compound, but I don't think he's in a cult." He shook his head. "How do you think Mom financed all the stuff in your new house? Dad bought everything, and he could do it a thousand times more before his bank would even think about calling."

I thought of Aunt Charlie, swiping a card in every store. Even though Mom was her sister, it had seemed a bit much at the time. "Why would he help us like that?"

"He and Uncle Justin went to college together. They were best friends."

"There's got to be more," I said.

"Oh, there's more. One night Dad sat in the library drinking, more than he should have. He said he owed everything to your father, even his life. It was ridiculous. He could drink, but we couldn't cuss?"

"What do you think he meant?"

Pade shrugged, but I had the feeling he knew more.

"Dad never talked about what happened in Colorado," I said, "beyond how he supposedly met Mom." There were too many secrets in our family, more than I could process. Dad's family, Mom's family, not to mention my own secret past. Looking down, I focused on a rock lodged in the bank. In my mind, I gripped the rock, pushing until… it broke free and rolled, landing against Pade's foot.

He spun to face me. "Did you hear what I said?"

I looked up at Pade, fighting a grin. I'd moved something with my mind. No doubt this time. My power had returned.

"So, we're there again." Frowning, he stood and walked away.

Watching him leave, my heart soared. Pade still

cared for me. The creases in his face told of the pain, of how he'd missed me. I'd hoped for this feeling, and yet in that same moment the torment of why we could never be filled my heart with dread. We were different—not just in name and family like he'd once insisted. He was from Earth and I was from another planet—one I must get back to. Loving Pade would only end in heartache for us both.

It was time to find Chase and show him I'd found my power.

If only I knew where to start.

CHAPTER FOUR

Another Tosh

I ran across the courtyard on my first day of class, wishing Mom and Dad hadn't fussed over every detail of the upcoming day.

"Wear your new sunscreen," Dad had said, reminding me of the new tube at the corner of my dresser. I'd looked at it for days, avoiding the thick goo that Dr. Baynor had insisted would keep me 'safe.' Whatever that meant. In the end, I'd rubbed it on, thrilled the smell had improved even if the stickiness seemed worse.

"Maybe she should stay home today," Dad said, looking to Mom. "Jes doesn't look one hundred percent yet. I can call out and stay with her."

Not in a million years, I thought.

"She'll be fine." Mom patted my cheek. "I'll talk with your new teachers. There's no reason we can't make everything easy for you this first day."

Nothing about this day would be easy.

It was déjà vu from a year ago.

The last bell rang as building three came into sight, but I froze when I noticed two girls near the entrance.

Rachelle stood, back against the building, in the shadow made where a metal roof overhung the brick wall. A figure leaned forward as she cowered, the girl's chin nearly six inches above Rachelle's fearful eyes.

Gripping the straps of my backpack, I ran to the wall of building three, mostly on my toes as I tried to keep out of sight. Along the wall, I flattened against the brick and eased to the corner, where I could inch around to see both girls.

From the side, this new girl looked as if she'd literally crawled off the cover of Sleeping Beauty and decided to enroll at Credence High. Besides the fact she towered above me, she couldn't have been more than a size two. Thick golden curls cascaded down her back, barely held at her neck by a black clip. Her face could have been made of porcelain, every angle a smooth finish that caused the light pink of her cheeks and eyelids to seem painted on. She pulled a pink and silver cardigan close to her chest, although sweat dripped down my cheeks.

Her voice was dainty, like a teacup that could be shattered with one touch, but underneath raged an anger that forced me to step back. Who was this girl?

"Brianna," Rachelle mumbled, "I'm sorry. No one cared for Leigh Ann more than I did."

"Don't you dare say her name," the girl hissed.

"Girls," said a voice and I noticed our principal, Dr. Greene, had opened one of the doors. "Get to class."

"Yes, sir." Brianna smiled at him. "Rachelle was just helping me find my first class."

Dr. Greene smiled. "Rachelle is one of many

wonderful students you'll meet at Credence High."

Brianna regarded Rachelle with a slight nod, but her smile didn't fade. "I'm good now. Thanks." She grabbed the backpack near her feet and walked through the door Dr. Greene held open.

"I'm in building five," Rachelle said, her voice nearly a whisper.

"Very well." He ducked back into building three.

As the door closed, I shot around the corner. "Are you okay?"

Rachelle's eyes widened, but she said nothing.

"Who was that girl?"

Rachelle glanced around the corner where I'd been hiding. "Brianna Lars."

"Is she—"

"No," Rachelle said. "You don't want to know anything about her." She grabbed my arm, pushing me toward the entrance. "Don't we share first block?"

I sighed. "History with Mr. Jones."

"Not anymore," she said. "Mr. Jones is out for surgery and won't be back for several weeks. There's a new teacher."

Great, I thought. It really was last year all over again. "Didn't you tell Dr. Greene your first class was in building five?" I struggled to keep up as Rachelle threw open the door of building three and nearly ran down the hall. From me?

"I lied to get rid of him," she said, over her shoulder.

"Who is Leigh Ann?" I asked.

Rachelle spun to face me, her voice razor sharp. "Don't ever ask me that again."

"But—"

"Stay out of it," Rachelle said. "You don't want to know this about me."

She didn't say another word. I ran behind her, slowing only as we stepped into history class.

The new teacher stood before a blackboard. I froze when she looked up from her podium and met my eyes. Déjà vu slapped me for the second time that day.

Her baggy pants and t-shirt were far from the formal attire Mrs. Pearson had worn on a daily basis. And her shoes—flat sandals were barely visible through the gap beneath the podium.

"Your names please," she said coldly.

"Rachelle Whitman," my friend replied.

She nodded, her eyes taking me in. "I am Mrs. Austen. And you are?"

I blinked, holding back a laugh. Mrs. Austen? As in Jane Austen, author of the beloved book Mrs. Pearson gave me? "Jessica Delaney."

"Good, find your seat Miss Delaney." She turned back to the board.

The way she said my name, with frost attached to each syllable, felt eerily reminiscent of a certain English teacher Bailey still hated.

Could the day get any stranger? She didn't look anything like Mrs. Pearson had. Her hair was dark, a mixture of brown and gold, and halfway down her back. She paused to push the jagged bangs from her eyes. She wore no glasses. And yet…

"Well?" she asked, pausing as she wrote a breakdown of our grades for the semester.

"Sorry," I muttered and lowered into a seat near the back of class. How had she managed to find a real chalkboard anyway? No teacher at Credence High had used a chalkboard since they'd removed the one from Mrs. Pearson's old class in the spring, opting for a white board instead.

Turning, I noticed a guy sat next to me. The gold highlights along his dark brown hair exactly matched the color of hers. He wore sunglasses, but the features of his face didn't match Chase in any way. His skin was a polished bronze and his muscles tight within the sleeves of his polo shirt. Larger than Chase, maybe even taller, he seemed to loom over the desk.

I watched him carefully, silently willing him to look up. His eyes never moved, as if frozen to the black binder beneath his pen.

The strange feeling returned, only this time it was back for good.

* * * * *

I picked at the pizza on my plate. If only the stupid computer had given Bailey first lunch. Stuck with second lunch, she'd used every fake cuss word she could conjure until we had to take opposite halls. I'd spend all year eating with Angel and Rachelle. She'd be alone.

When the bell finally rang, I gave up on the pizza.

"Got to meet Skip," Angel said as she ran from the lunchroom.

People rushed around us, but Rachelle lifted her backpack as if she planned to stay and eat lunch again. "Angel is sharing a locker with Skip."

The sadness in her voice reminded me of Brianna. "Do you want to share a locker?"

Rachelle stared at me. "What about Bailey?"

I shrugged. "We can all share."

"I'll share with Pade," Bailey said, appearing at my side.

"Share with your brother?" Rachelle did a double take. "What about Terrance?"

Bailey shook her head. "They're still not talking."

I looked at the pizza, but my appetite had not returned. "Is anything the same as last year?"

"Yeah." Rachelle stood. "This school still sucks."

Bailey watched as Rachelle pushed through the doors. "Chase is still gone."

"I'm sorry," I said, unsettled by how she'd nearly read my mind.

"Don't be," Bailey said. "I called him, remember? I guess I got what I deserved."

"Don't say that."

She sighed. "Don't you have another class?"

"Yeah, pre-cal."

"Stuck in a class where your mom's the teacher? Chase used to say that super sucked. I guess you better hurry since Aunt Rainey will be worried." Bailey smiled. "You can share a locker with Rachelle. I get it—Angel won't part with Skip. You'll probably get bottom row. I'll make sure Pade gets us the one right above."

Seeing Pade every day at the locker—that's just what I needed. "Maybe this isn't a good idea."

"Trust me, Pade will be relieved. No one is talking to him. It seems nobody at Credence High likes people who abandon their best friends."

"But it wasn't his fault," I said. Bailey's father had insisted on taking her and Pade back to Colorado for the spring semester. How could Terrance think Pade abandoned him when Pade didn't have a choice? I sighed as the answer became clear. I'd felt the same way for months after Bailey left.

Bailey stared at me. "Tell me you don't feel that way."

I met her eyes. "I don't."

Her lips formed a sad smile. "Don't lie to make me feel better."

Gripping my backpack, I lifted the strap over my arm. "I might have felt that way in the spring, but not now."

"Thanks," she said, but I could tell she still doubted my words.

Trashing the pizza, I stepped outside the door, but took a last look at Bailey. She reached in her bag and pulled out a paperback book. Bailey was going to *read* during lunch? Pade entered at a side door and took the quickest path to her table. People around him whispered, pointed, and one member of the football team even raised his middle finger behind Pade's back.

The sight disturbed me, but I wasn't sure why. I'd been teased and tormented at schools across the country. We'd only moved thirty times, and I personally knew three times that many nasty people existed in the world. But Pade was different. In seventeen years, he'd probably never been teased.

Six months ago, I would have loved to see him spend a single day understanding how I felt about Tosh. Now that the whole school had developed a hatred for Pade, I felt…

Pity? Remorse? Or maybe just a sense of understanding. I didn't hate Pade. Watching the tense look on his face made me want to run to class. Or walk to the table and hug his neck.

I stared at the football player, concentrating on the

carton of milk next to his plate. I held my breath, waiting for movement. When he reached for his drink, the carton tipped over, spilling milk across the table and into his lap. Yelling, the guy stood and did a little dance, and Bailey pointed and insisted Pade look. I smiled, even though Pade would never know I'd caused the excitement.

I'd almost reached Mom's class when an alarm began to wail. Lights flashed along the hall. Before I could reach her door, someone came around the corner and crashed into me.

"Damn it." Ronald Pitts pushed me aside. "I was never here."

As he ran down the hall, I rounded the corner and noticed the fire alarm pulled to my side. Doors began to open and students filed out, some running with teachers screaming from behind.

A weird thought flashed in my head. I could un-pull the fire alarm. I slammed my palm against my forehead. No, that would mean way more attention than I'd ever need.

Behind me, a voice boomed. "What is going on?"

Turning, I looked up at Dr. Greene.

His words were slow, controlled. "Jessica Delaney, please tell me you did not pull that fire alarm."

Mom appeared next to Dr. Greene. "Is this a fake?"

"Apparently so," he said, still staring at me. "Did you see who pulled it?"

"No," I said, but couldn't stop the waver in my voice.

"Was anyone else in the hall?" he asked.

"Joel," Mom said, "please, lower your voice. This excitement is probably too much for Jes as it is." She turned to a student. "I'll be out in a minute."

"Who did you see?" Dr. Greene demanded.

"Ronald Pitts," I whispered, but he heard despite the voices rushing by.

"Ronald?" Mom looked doubtful.

"We'll find out." Dr. Greene headed down the hall.

Mom put an arm around me. "You didn't really pull it, did you? I know taking my class will be strange, but I promise not to call on you. Much."

Chase had hated his mom's class. Jeez, he was my brother and I still thought of Mrs. Pearson as only *his* mom. But was she really his mom? Maybe it had all been a lie.

"Jes," Mom said, bringing me back to reality. "Let's go get everyone. Looks like this is going to be a first day to remember."

Or forget. I cringed imagining what Ronald might do when he discovered I ratted him out.

* * * * *

On Friday afternoon, I kneeled at my locker and sighed as exhaustion screamed from every muscle. Although I'd never admit it to Mom and Dad, maybe going back to school so soon after the hospital had been too much.

Ronald had been suspended after Dr. Greene convinced him to admit pulling the fire alarm. He couldn't step foot onto campus until Tuesday, which might be a good day for me to claim the first week of school was too much. Dad would buy it, even if Mom didn't. In fact, I might not have to fake it.

Pade walked up and leaned against the lockers next to me.

I looked up at him. "Want me to move?"

"Take your time," he said. "I don't really need to use the locker."

Then why was he standing there? Since I didn't have any homework for the weekend, I pulled the books from my bag and stacked them next to Rachelle's. I struggled to get the books to stand neatly, but Pade offered no help as he stared.

"Have you ever been in love?" he asked.

I dropped the book in my hand. "What?"

"Not a silly crush in-love, but full-blown can't live without someone love?"

"Maybe," I said, but trapped under his gaze I wasn't so sure. Had I ever really loved Pade or were my feelings for him just a silly crush?

Pade rolled his eyes. "Someone from this planet?"

The tone of his voice irritated me, and I couldn't pinpoint why. Was it his new 'me against the world' attitude or the fact he still thought I liked Chase? Maybe it was better for him to keep thinking I had a thing for Chase. Closing my backpack, I slammed the locker door. "Maybe. Or maybe not."

His eyes narrowed, betraying his fury, but in the next moment the anger faded and he stepped closer. "This part about you drives me crazy."

"I think I loved someone once but he left. Can we not talk about this anymore?"

"Don't make that face," Pade said, in a half-tortured, half-taunting voice. "It makes me want to kiss you."

I looked around. Bailey and Rachelle stood beyond the lockers, whispering, just close enough to hear our words. Embarrassment burned in my face. My hand rose to smack his cheek.

Pade grabbed my wrist. "Go out with me Saturday."

"You can't be serious." My parents would freak.

"I'm having lunch with Terrance and Mia. We still haven't *talked* since I've been back. I told Mia it was a waste of time, but she insisted."

"Maybe Terrance wants to talk."

"I won't get my hopes up." He pulled me forward. "Please, Jes, I need you there."

I stared into his eyes, felt his gentle pleading. "What if Terrance wants to kick your head in? Am I supposed to sit and watch?"

"If that's what it takes. I deserve whatever Terrance has to say. And if he throws a couple of punches—at least I might feel a little better about how I treated him."

"I don't want to see you get beat up, even if you do deserve it. What does it matter if I'm there?"

"I'd be lying if I said I knew myself."

"Okay," I said, but stood in disbelief my own lips had formed the word.

"Good." He released my wrist. "We're meeting at that Italian restaurant downtown. Remember where we went for my birthday?"

"Of course," I whispered.

He nodded, acknowledging the memories that crowded the depths of my heart. The flash in his eyes was unmistakable.

I had to say something to break the silence. "You still can't pick me up for a date."

"Bailey will work out the details." He smiled and started down the hall. "She's the best planner I know."

Bailey and Rachelle giggled as they approached. Since Bailey would probably spend the night, I figured it was going to be a long one.

CHAPTER FIVE

Secrets Discovered

After a long night of assuring Bailey I wasn't still in love with her brother, she finally gave up on playing matchmaker. I'd agreed to the lunch, and she'd worked out all of the details, promising not to keep asking about me and Pade. I got dressed and followed Bailey to her house. Thankfully, Pade was nowhere in sight.

"I've got the perfect outfit," she said as we entered her bedroom.

"Have you changed your mind about the restaurant?" I asked.

She walked into the closet. "No, I'm still meeting Rachelle next door. Pade will just have to fill me in later."

I sat on her bed, tugging the sleeves of my windbreaker up to my elbows. The heat outside was intense, but I didn't want anyone to hear my teeth chatter in the sub-zero restaurant. "Do you think Terrance will forgive Pade?"

"Terrance feels abandoned," she said, her words

muffled.

"Tell me something I don't know."

Bailey shoved the hangers, as if suddenly impatient. "I talked to Lauren."

Stunned, I scrambled off the bed. "As in Chase's Lauren?"

She stepped out of the closet and pointed a finger at me. "Don't ever call her that."

Lauren McCall, who'd never bothered to return any of my messages? "Is she still in New York City?"

"Yes, but she doesn't know where Chase is or if he's ever coming back." Bailey held up a sequined tank. "Too much?"

Faced with the magnitude of her words, I couldn't reply, only shook my head. *If* he was coming back?

"Hey," she said. "Don't look so sad."

I swallowed the pain in my throat.

Bailey put an arm around my shoulders, hugging me close. "If you miss Chase half as much as I do, then I feel for you."

"He was your boyfriend."

"Yeah," she said, "until he took a spaceship back to his home planet." She laughed bitterly. "I thought going to Colorado would help me forget."

"It didn't work?" I asked, holding back the tears.

"No. Pade hates how much I miss Chase. I suspect he hates how much you miss Chase even more."

"I need to find him. There's so much I didn't say before he left." If only I'd told him the truth about my dreams.

"Well, at least you got to say goodbye. I was unconscious, remember?" She pulled back and met my eyes. "I've never forgiven you for that. And you never said how you convinced him you weren't the girl they were searching for."

That night came back in a flood, pushing the tears to my eyes. The guards at the mall had used a paralyzer on us. After I could move again, Chase and his mother had confronted me, insisting I was the missing girl they'd been searching for. The lost girl from their planet. I'd showed them the articles about Jessica Naples to prove I couldn't be her. Chase had begged me to tell the truth, to admit my dreams. If only I'd told them I remembered the night I hid on the spaceship twelve years ago.

"It wasn't so difficult," I said. Especially not with the lies my parents had told.

She looked me over carefully. "Do you still want to find Chase?"

"Yes."

"Good." She went back into the closet. "Dad had a great computer. Even though he swore to cut the cord if I contacted anyone in Credence, he never said I couldn't email someone in New York."

I laughed in a nervous burst.

"Seriously, I researched every alien sighting and supposed abduction case for the last year. I took notes."

"You've never taken notes on anything."

"I've got a box wrapped in a hundred feet of duct tape. It's one of the few things I insisted on bringing back when we got the call about you." She lowered her eyes. "I hid the box out back in the shed. Mom never goes in there because of all the dust. She always sends me or Pade."

"Were there any more abductions?"

"None that seemed to fit Chase's motive. Lauren

insisted he went back home to stay, but I figured if they didn't find the girl they'd keep looking. Don't you think?"

Or maybe they had found her. "How much time do we have?"

"Mom wants to see us before we leave. She'll be home from the hospital in twenty minutes, but if we hurry…"

"Then let's go."

The metal building sat at the back of their property along a fence with a wild cherry tree that made a screeching sound with every blast of steamy wind. We crossed the empty lawn, a layer of grass now evenly spread where a pool once sat.

Despite the heat, I pulled my jacket closer as I eyed a spider's web in the window. "Aunt Charlie doesn't clean out here?"

Bailey laughed and pointed at the spider. "Mom hates bugs. That's why she always sends me or Pade."

She held up the key ring, sliding a silver key into the lock at the door. Bailey turned the key, jiggling it before the lock gave way. She grunted as she shoved, but the door didn't budge.

I leaned my shoulder against the door and between the two of us it gave way. Coughing, I waved the cloud of dust that exploded in my face.

"See why Mom would never find the box in here?"

My eyes adjusted to the darkness as we stepped into the shed. I scanned row after row of boxes piled up to the ceiling. Some plastic totes were marked with tape, some boxes had writing like 'Christmas' on the side. All seemed perfectly normal covered with their own layer of dust, until one box on the top shelf caught my eye.

The box was blue, or was it black? I squinted, wishing the window allowed more than the tiny beam of light. It looked like a shoe box, stacked on top of two others. It was definitely blue. No, it couldn't be. And yet, I moved closer until the rubber band came into focus.

Bailey was talking about Lauren again. She'd lifted a box covered with tape. I climbed onto a plastic tote and reached for the shelf, praying the tote would hold my weight.

"What are you doing?" a voice asked.

I spun, nearly falling from the tote, as Pade grabbed my arms and steadied me. "Nothing," I said.

Pade grinned. "You were reaching for something." He looked up. "That box maybe?"

"No," I said.

"Looks like a shoe box, but I don't remember what's in it."

My past, I thought, realizing this might be my only chance. It had to be the box Mom showed me last fall, with all of the newspaper clippings and my adoption papers. It even had the rubber band she'd wrapped around it.

Laughing, Pade climbed up and grabbed the box. "Got it," he said, breaking the rubber with a single tug.

"No," I screamed.

He stopped laughing to stare at me. The box slipped from his hand and crashed to the floor at my feet. The top split from the box, spilling the articles and yellowed documents across the floor.

Bailey reached down and grabbed a newspaper clipping.

"Give me that," I said, reaching for the page, but she spun toward the window.

"Wow, who is this girl gripping her teddy bear like the end of the world is coming?" Her smile faded. "Oh my god, her name is Jessica. Is this you?" she asked as Pade ripped the page from her hand.

Could I lie? Was there any point? "Yes," I said, on the brink of tears.

Pade scanned the article. "This is from a paper in New York City. This Jessica was kidnapped." He looked me over critically. "How can you be her?"

I dropped to my knees and gathered all of the papers into a stack. "I came from New York. That's where Dad found me—on a highway at midnight. He nearly ran me over with that old Ford we used to have."

Pade crossed his arms. "What were you doing on a highway at night?"

"No one knows for sure, but they think I ran away."

"You don't remember?" Bailey asked, her eyes wide.

"Not really," I lied. In truth, I still couldn't remember how I ended up on that road, staring into Dad's headlights. "It was so long ago."

"But I thought you came from Canton," she said. "We talked about this…"

I looked up at Bailey. "They made me lie all these years. No one could know about me or the reporters would come after us again."

"Again?" Pade didn't seem convinced. "What happened to your real parents?"

"No one has seen them since the night I was found. Turns out they weren't really so desperate to find me after all."

"Shit," Bailey said. "They just left you? That's super messed up." She looked to Pade. "Makes you think Dad's not so bad."

Pade was still staring at me. "You've kept this secret all these years?"

"Dad made me promise not to tell anyone."

"Crap," Bailey said, looking out the tiny window. "Mom's home." She spun around. "We'll have to talk about this later."

Taking the box from my shaking hands, Pade helped me force all of the papers inside and close the lid. "Should I put it back?"

I didn't want to let the box out of my sight, but with Pade watching so closely, I nodded. "For now."

* * * * *

Bailey dusted off her arms as she stepped into the kitchen. Aunt Charlie stood near the fridge, reaching for the coffee pot.

"Give me ten minutes to change," Bailey said, running past her mom for the stairs.

"Bailey Sanders," Aunt Charlie said, "you get rid of those nasty clothes this instant."

Bailey laughed as she reached the top.

Something had been bugging me ever since Chase left. I crossed the floor and stood at Aunt Charlie's side. "Why don't you have any pictures on the wall?"

"Excuse me?" she asked, nearly dropping the coffee.

I reached out to steady her. "Most people hang pictures. Why are we different?"

She poured coffee into a white cup trimmed with flowers, leaving a full inch for creamer. "I notice you said 'we.' What makes you think *we're* different?"

"Angel and Rachelle—their walls are full of

pictures."

"Have you asked your mom about this?"

"Mom would never understand. She acts like moving thirty times and never talking about the past is normal."

She seemed to consider. "Lorraine probably understands what you've gone through better than anyone."

"Why don't you have pictures of your mom and dad?"

"Daddy used to keep pictures of us all, but everything we had burned up in a fire."

"At the old blue house?" I asked.

Aunt Charlie smiled weakly and waved me into the living room, to the overstuffed leather couch. She sat down next to a table where she placed the cup and patted the spot beside her. "We had another house, before the one at the lake."

Another house? "Mom hasn't said anything about another house."

"She was younger then. We don't talk about that house because of the fire."

I laughed bitterly as I took the seat next to her. "Mom definitely never mentioned a fire."

"Jes, you're not the only one with a traumatic past. Lorraine had a twin sister. There were three of us."

My mouth gaped open. "What happened?"

"I'll tell you, but only because your mom hasn't been able to. I want you to understand it's not that she's been purposely hiding her past from you—she just doesn't want to remember it."

Mom hide her past? *My* blue box, *my* entire past, was tucked away on a forgotten shelf in Aunt Charlie's shed. "Do you know about New York?" I asked carefully.

Aunt Charlie reached for the coffee, bringing it to her lips, and closed her eyes. "Three little girls. Charlene, Lorraine, and Darla."

We sat in silence while she took a long sip, as if the cup was really a bottle of cough syrup she couldn't force down. The cup was half-empty before she spoke again.

"I'm sure you've heard twins can run in a family. Twins ran on my mother's side and even though the gene skipped me, Lorraine was born with a twin. She and Darla were identical."

"Like Danny and Collin?" I asked.

She opened her eyes. "Like Danny and Collin. I was seven when the house burned. Lorraine and Darla were five."

The same age as I was when Dad found me.

"There was a storm that night—electrical. Lightning hit the house and started the fire. Daddy pulled me out of bed while Momma went for Lorraine and Darla. I remember the smoke and waking up in a coughing fit. Daddy threw me on the ground and went back in. By the time I could catch my breath, he and Momma pushed through the door with Lorraine and Darla. Lorraine was burned, but you can barely see the scars now. Darla was burned over sixty percent of her body. Lorraine made it through, but Darla died a week later in the hospital.

"All the pictures were gone, but it was probably for the best. When Lorraine woke up, she cried for Darla. For weeks, she wouldn't speak to anyone. I tried to reach her, anything to ease the pain, but Momma said I couldn't understand the loss she felt. I never had a twin."

Aunt Charlie took my hand. "Months later, Daddy took a picture of me and Lorraine and framed it over the fireplace in the blue house. The next morning, the frame was shattered. Momma cleaned it up and told Daddy not to take any more. No one ever said anything else about pictures to Lorraine."

I thought of the phone I'd broken and how Mom never mentioned it to me. "Did she talk to you about the picture?"

"Years later, but Lorraine and I have never been close. Not like she was with Darla. We've gone months and even years without talking. I didn't know about Justin's sickness until a few months before you moved here. Otherwise, I would've been at the hospital, holding her hand through every treatment, and not just the last few."

"You went to see her in Atlanta?"

"Yes."

I looked at the stairs. Bailey would be coming down any minute.

"I'd do anything for my sister," Aunt Charlie said. "She's the main reason I never moved to Colorado. I always knew she'd come back here."

And after all the years, we had. "She always talked about Credence like she'd never want to live anywhere else. But then we moved all over the country."

"Lorraine had her reasons." Aunt Charlie put an arm around me and hugged me close. "And yes, I know all about New York."

* * * * *

"So," Pade said, "all this time you were adopted in New York? You guys never even lived in Canton?"

As he drove, I'd spent the last fifteen minutes telling the whole story. I didn't want to go over it again. I turned around to look at Bailey. "It's how I knew for sure I wasn't from Chase's planet."

She shook her head, maybe even sighed in relief. "I can't believe Aunt Rainey and Uncle Justin have lied all these years. And they made you lie?"

"Yeah."

Pade slammed his hands against the steering wheel. "Our family is so messed up." He turned to me. "You really liked Chase, didn't you?"

My blood ran cold. "What are you asking?"

"We all knew you connected with him. You had something special, admit it."

Bailey punched the back of his seat. "Shut up, Pade!"

He turned down the radio.

"It isn't what you think," I whispered.

Pade laughed, a sound that irritated me. "Give me *one* good reason why it isn't."

Chase is my brother. "He was my friend. That's all," I added, unable to keep the sorrow from my voice.

"Okay then," Pade said, maneuvering the jeep into the parking lot as the restaurant came into sight. "Let's talk about lunch. You know this isn't going to be good."

"Make Terrance understand," Bailey said.

Pade snickered. "Terrance doesn't forgive or forget."

I stared through the tinted glass at my side, which made the clouds seem darker than normal. The threat of rain felt ominous after the tone of Pade's voice.

Terrance would forgive and forget. He must. They'd been friends since first grade.

The jeep slowed as we approached a couple of speed bumps, but not enough to keep me from bouncing in the seat.

Bailey hit his seat again. "Jeez, Pade, kill us all now."

He pulled into an empty spot and turned off the jeep. Pade leaned back against the seat and closed his eyes. For a moment, no one said a word. The radio continued with a sad country song, too low to make out the words.

I thought of a time when I would have been thrilled to ride in a camouflage jeep, especially one with less than five thousand miles and matching seats. Not seat covers, real stitched camouflage with the power to heat and cool. The chrome that traced the radio seemed to glow from the blue lights.

Pade reached for his door. "Maybe if the jeep tears up, Dad will get the idea."

Bailey climbed out behind him. "At least for now we have a ride."

"She's right," I said. "This jeep is way better than my ride."

Pade nodded and squeezed my hand. "Thanks."

"For what?" I asked.

"For being you." He laughed. "Do you consider this a date?"

His words stunned me, but I said the first answer that came to mind. "Yes." For the first time in weeks, a weight lifted and I laughed with him. I reached for the door.

"Wait." He circled the jeep and stopped at my side, opening the door. "Since this is really a date, I want it to be right."

"How cute," Bailey said. Her words held sarcasm, but her eyes betrayed a happiness I hadn't seen since before she left for Colorado. "If you two are good, I'm going to meet Rachelle."

"Sure," Pade said. His grin faded as he looked toward the Italian restaurant.

Low, romantic music played as we stepped into the dark room. A silver-haired woman in a long dress smiled from behind a podium. "How many?"

I glanced around at the empty tables. Pade opened his mouth, but no words emerged.

"We're meeting someone," I said.

"Party of four?" she asked. When we both nodded, the woman led us to a table at the back of the restaurant.

Mia looked up and waved us over. Terrance glared at the menu, silent as Pade pulled out a chair for me.

"Thought you might have forgotten," Mia said.

"Or went back to Colorado," Terrance added.

Pade sat down. "I deserved that."

"Man, you have no idea." Terrance slammed the menu on the table. "Six months without a 'hey, what's up.' You can't tell me your dad kept you from calling."

Tell him the truth, I thought.

"I heard you came to Credence in July," Terrance said. "Why didn't you call?"

Pade glanced at Mia but didn't look at me. "Not sure what you're talking about."

"Yeah, lie some more," Terrance said, his words blazing. "What's the point of telling the truth now?"

"You're my friend," Pade said, softly. "I never meant to abandon you. How can I make this up?"

Terrance looked at the table. "Coach says he had

you a jersey made, just in case you change your mind."

"I haven't changed my mind."

"Credence needs you. All the guys need you. Your arm, man—you throw better than anyone I've ever seen."

Pade's voice was controlled. "I'm not playing this year."

"Why the hell not?" Terrance yelled, jumping to his feet.

Mia grabbed Terrance's arm and pulled him back into the seat. "People are staring."

"What people?" he snarled, sweeping his hand around the room. "This place is like the stadium will be, after we *lose* every game."

"Please," Mia begged, "can't we just eat?"

A waitress appeared and I let out a nervous sigh. Her apron had a button with a yellow smiley face. How appropriate.

"What you guys want to drink?" she asked.

"Whatever," Terrance mumbled.

"Tea," Mia said, "with lots of sugar."

"How about the 'Long Island' kind?" Terrance asked.

The waitress grinned. "Yeah, right."

As she walked away, Terrance stood, brushing away Mia's arm. "I need a few minutes."

Pade watched as he headed for the front door.

"Tell him," Mia hissed.

"What?" Pade asked.

"Whatever it takes to make this right."

"I don't know if anything can make this right."

Mia looked at me. "Did you forgive the disappearing act?"

I looked at Pade. His eyes questioned mine, as if he honestly wasn't sure. "Yes."

"Okay." She reached for Pade's hand. "If Jes can forgive you for leaving, why can't Terrance?"

Pade put his hands in his lap. "It wasn't just that I left."

"I know," Mia said. "He wants you to play football. No, he *needs* you to play football."

"Terrance is great on his own."

"You don't get it. Terrance doesn't have what you have. He doesn't have a gift for throwing the ball, and he doesn't have a dad who's loaded."

"I can't help that," Pade said.

Mia's voice faded, almost to a whisper. "He's counting on a scholarship—a football scholarship. The only way he has a chance of getting noticed is if Credence goes to state. For that to happen, you'd have to be throwing the ball."

"He'll get a scholarship," Pade said.

"Maybe," Mia admitted. "But Terrance doesn't see that. All he sees is the fact you left him hanging, which hurt. He believes you ran to your rich father, who could probably send you to any college. Is he right?"

"Yes," Pade said.

"You won't play football, which doesn't just hurt his feelings. Now you're killing his dreams. Why?"

"You wouldn't understand."

Mia stood. "You're right, I don't. Something about you has changed, Pade Sanders, and not for the good. I suggest you stay out of Terrance's way. He's likely to have the whole school ready to fight you soon. Is that more important than your secrets?"

Pade didn't say a word as Mia followed Terrance's

path.

I placed a hand on Pade's arm. "Why not tell them about your dad?"

"They wouldn't understand. Plus, I don't want them to know I'm related to such a black-hearted bastard. Anyone with half a brain would run the other way."

"You told me the truth and I understood. I didn't run."

He smiled with an irony that twisted my stomach. "Bailey told you the truth. I wasn't ever going to tell you."

I felt as if the breath had been knocked from my chest. "But I thought—"

"Whatever you thought about me, you were wrong."

CHAPTER SIX

New Friends

On Monday, I skipped hanging out and went straight to first block. My feelings were still raw from Saturday, and I couldn't take a chance on seeing Pade again so soon. He knew the secret about Jessica Naples. For two nights, my thoughts had been tortured by what he might think of me, of my parents. We'd had lunch as a family on Sunday, but he'd avoided every opportunity to look my way.

I spent the ride to school again going over the scene from the restaurant. Terrance's face had been marred by pain and anger. Mia was shocked at Pade's unwillingness to help his friend. The whole school would hate Pade. I should hate him after admitting his plans to never tell me the truth.

As I hoped, the new guy was already at his desk. The class was silent, empty except for the two of us. I dropped in the desk next to his and scooted closer.

He stopped writing in the black binder and closed it, but didn't raise his eyes.

"What's your name?" I asked.

After what seemed like hours, he finally spoke. "Joe."

I pulled back a little at his deep voice. "Which is short for?"

He raised an eyebrow. "Joseph." He shifted in his seat to look at me, giving me his full attention. "How did you know my name wasn't Joe?"

"Just a guess."

Joe looked down at my desk. "I don't like people in my personal space."

Wow, he was serious. I slid my desk away from him. "I've sat next to you for days, but you haven't said a word."

"Sometimes people talk too much." He pointed to a cluster of girls who laughed as they entered the room. "I'm not social like they are. Why are *you* talking to me?"

Good question. Although something about this guy reeked of Chase, his face and voice both told a different story. Maybe I was wrong. "Sorry if I offended you, but I thought you might need a friend."

This time both eyebrows rose. "You want to hang out with me?"

"Why not?" I asked.

To my surprise, he smiled. "You'll change your mind."

"Maybe."

He collected himself and leaned closer to me. "I'm not the best-friend kind of guy."

"Since I'm not a guy, I wouldn't know."

He inched slightly closer. "I'd break your heart."

I shrugged. "Maybe I'm not the heart-break kind of girl."

"I hate this school."

"So do I on most days."

Joe cleared his throat. "I've been in prison."

"My whole life is a prison."

The confidence in his face wavered. "You said that like you believe it."

"I do. I'd give anything for a way out."

"Find your seats," growled a voice from the doorway.

I looked up as Mrs. Austen crossed to the front of the room. Other students filed into the class, including Rachelle.

"Miss Delaney, must you block the aisle?"

Scrambling to my feet, I pulled my desk back in place. "Sorry."

Her voice could have frozen Lake Credence solid. "See that it does not happen again. Next time I will give everyone an assigned seat."

"She's mean," I whispered to Joe.

"You don't know the half of it," he muttered. Turning back to his desk, Joe opened the binder and started writing again. "I can't help you," he added, staring straight ahead.

"Yet," he whispered, but I looked at the board as if I never heard.

* * * * *

"See anything I missed?" Bailey asked.

I shook my head and glanced over the pages spread across my bed. News articles about mysterious disappearances. Pictures of UFOs. Interviews with people claiming to be victims of alien abductions.

"Reminds me of the *X-Files*," Bailey said.

"What?" I asked.

"Don't say you've never seen that show—it runs all the time on one of those sci-fi channels. Super cute guy? His sister was abducted by aliens or at least that's what they always hinted."

I shrugged.

"You should watch more TV. In one episode, the aliens were experimenting on human—"

"We almost got kidnapped by aliens. Why would I want to watch that?"

She grinned. "Good point, although I never got the impression Chase planned to dissect our brains." Handing me a stack of emails, she pulled herself up from the bed. "That's everything from Lauren."

Four conversations, the last dated back in May. "She says Chase never contacted her again."

"Did you read the second page?"

I flipped back to the email, not realizing there had been another page. Scanning each line, my heart nearly stopped at the end.

Jes wasn't the girl. That's why Chase is never coming back.

"What's wrong?" Bailey asked.

"Nothing," I stammered. "Nothing is wrong."

"You're not her, but you knew that."

I swallowed hard. "Yeah."

"Something is wrong," she said.

Swallowing again, I pushed the sob back into my throat. I had to be the girl Chase was searching for. I remembered that night. I'd regained my power. Lauren was wrong.

If only I could tell Bailey the truth about my past or how I thought Chase might actually be back in

Credence. "I'm fine. I just miss Chase."

"Me too."

I gathered the papers. "This was a waste of time."

"Jes?"

Looking up, I arranged the pages in a neat stack. "I'm good. Promise."

"Did you tell Chase the truth about New York?"

"It's how I convinced Chase and Mrs. Pearson to let us go."

Bailey stared at me. "I've wondered why they went to all the trouble to kidnap us and then just dropped us back at the mall."

"Dad made me promise to keep the secret about Jessica Naples, but it wasn't worth us being dragged across the sky to another planet."

"Good thing you came clean to Chase," she said, though her voice seemed nowhere near forgiving.

* * * * *

Darkness surrounded me as I stared at the ceiling. No one stirred beyond my bedroom door. The clock on the nightstand had glowed eleven-thirty the last time I looked. If only sleep would come, but no way could I stop thinking about Chase.

This new guy couldn't be Chase. He'd pushed me away, complained about me in his 'personal space,' and then actually seemed worried when I painted him a picture of what my life had become without Chase. Between his odd emotions and the new teacher's familiar cold words, I found it hard to believe Chase and Mrs. Pearson hadn't returned. But what kept them away for so long? And why wasn't he in any hurry to tell me now?

My brain felt ready to explode. It was enough thinking Chase was being held against his will, denied the chance to return to Earth. But what if they'd been here all along?

The creek—maybe hearing the rushing water would clear my head. I closed my eyes and pictured myself near the bank. Opening my eyes, I let out a frustrated sigh. White plaster still hung above me.

I closed my eyes and thought of Chase, of the night I'd run away. I'd pictured myself on that platform a thousand times since January. Moving small objects with my mind had become a simple task in the last month, but I still hadn't managed to zap my whole body somewhere else. Pooling my emotions—fear for Chase, hatred for him possibly being so close, eagerness to see him—I opened my eyes, this time to a black canvas speckled with a million tiny lights.

Water splashed and gurgled to my side. Above me the moon hung in the sky, watching, welcoming me back to my favorite place.

Beneath my back was a bed of grass and leaves that had fallen. As I struggled to sit, the leaves crunched beneath me. The air was hot, no doubt more so since my bedroom enjoyed the advantage of our air conditioner, but it smelled fresh and wide open. My eyes adjusted to the night slowly, but I was in no hurry.

My heart swelled with the knowledge I'd finally used my gift for more than just a task my hands could accomplish. Sure, I was less than two miles from home, but I'd teleported myself here. TELEPORTED MYSELF. I threw my hands in the air and danced all the way to the water. Over and over, I told myself I'd used my power. Me. Jes Delaney. Who would ever believe me?

When I reached the bank, I sat on a rock and slid my bare feet into the water. My toes tingled against the smooth rocks, cold despite the rush of blood in my veins. Moonlight glittered across the rocks and water, reminding me why this place was so special. There was a beauty I didn't quite understand, but I knew one thing for sure. I didn't fear the water. I'd never feared water.

I took a deep breath, still unable to believe I'd finally wielded the same power as Chase. My power. Perhaps the gift never really left me. Maybe getting sick had released something inside of me. Or it could have been fate. The fortune teller at the fair had said my power would keep me safe.

But keep me safe from what?

A low growl came from bushes across the creek. I froze as the branches rustled. Closing my eyes, I pictured myself back in my bedroom.

Panic gripped my chest as the growl deepened. I opened my eyes as the branches rustled again. Chase's words from the night we sat on the rocks raced through my head.

When I'm scared, my powers don't always work.

I scrambled back from the rocks as an animal burst into the moonlight. It was a wolf, maybe a dog. No, the snarling beast that stalked toward me must be a coyote. The animal lowered its head, shoulders bulging with each step, baring a full mouth of razor-sharp teeth as it inched closer. Black lines formed a mask around the eyes and down to the black nose. A long shadow stretched across the creek, reaching my toes as huge yellow eyes focused on mine.

My heart raced. I jumped to my feet, tracing the dirt road in the moonlight. Running ahead, my lungs burned as I struggled to catch my breath. Feet scratched the ground behind me, barely making a sound as claws almost flew over the rocks. The air only amplified the deep breathing that closed the gap behind me with every second.

Another growl raged through the night.

My foot caught the edge of a rock.

I fell sideways, landing on my hip. Covering my face, I prayed with every ounce of strength I had left.

When I lowered my hands, the darkness of cold, stale air surrounded me. Had I imagined the animal, almost in range to tear my head off?

Looking down, I barely made out dirt lodged beneath my nails. Dad had warned me not to go to that creek many times.

Only one word summed up my feelings under the glare of that animal.

Powerless.

* * * * *

History class the next morning felt like a marathon run of a TV show I never wanted to watch in the first place. There was the usual boring lecture and then our teacher asked someone to read passages, no surprise. She wrote on the board and called every name in the room except for Joe's. When the bell rang, I looked at the empty desk next to me.

Mrs. Austen didn't raise her eyes as I approached her desk.

"Yes, Miss Delaney?"

"Let me guess, Joe didn't feel well today."

She paused in her writing and looked up at me. "Who?"

I rolled my eyes. "The guy who sits next to me."

She stared at me, a curious look on her face.

For a moment, I stood in silence, but as students made their way in for second block, I realized she didn't plan to respond.

"Fine." I stomped toward the door.

My anger simmered during second block and lunch, rising another notch each time I thought of Chase and Mrs. Pearson. Were they playing games with me now? Did they think I wouldn't figure out it was them or were the connections merely in my mind?

"Did you hear what I said about Skip?"

I nodded to Angel when in reality I neither heard nor cared. Rachelle sat next to her, picking at a plate of grilled chicken salad that almost overflowed to the tray underneath. She looked up, frowning, but didn't say a word.

Wasting no time when the bell rang, I headed for the exit and crashed into Tosh in the doorway.

"Sorry," she said, backing up until recognition flashed in her eyes. "Jes!" Tosh grabbed my arms and pulled me outside.

She wore a T-shirt that said *Bahamas* and covered more skin than any other shirt she'd worn. Her red hair had been tamed into a single white scrunchy that made her makeup-free face... pretty. No wonder I hadn't picked her out of the crowd last week.

Shocked by her genuine tone, I hesitated as she pulled me into a corner near one of the counselor's offices. I froze when she threw her arms around my neck, gripping me in bear hug.

Had Tosh Henley been body-snatched and swapped with an alien? Was the real Tosh on a spaceship circling Earth? I giggled at the thought of Tosh being taken, but it was more of a nervous response to how close we stood. The arms around my neck could easily tighten in a second, leaving me to gasp for air.

"I'm so glad you came out of the coma," she said and released me. "You had everyone in Credence worried." Concern spread across her face as she noticed mine. "Did I grip too hard? Bailey said you were still weak…"

She'd been talking to Bailey? "I never had a problem surviving your grip before."

Her face fell. "I'm sorry, Jes." Tosh stepped back and eyed me with an uneasiness that didn't suit her. "I thought maybe I'd hurt you."

"You? Hurt me?" I asked with sarcasm.

She gave a pitiful laugh. "You're right, but I can't take that back."

"If you could—"

"Yes," she said. "I get we can't be friends. Bailey seems to have gotten over hating me; that will have to be enough for now."

We stared at each other. Maybe she was hoping for more from me, but I couldn't offer her friendship. Not Tosh. Not after how she bullied me. Eventually, she gave up and walked to the table where Bailey and Pade usually sat. As I watched through the doors, Bailey and Pade entered from the side door to the cafeteria and went straight to Tosh.

Jealousy welled inside of me. How could Bailey and Pade eat lunch with Tosh? The trio seemed in their own world as Tosh's lips moved and Bailey laughed. Pade grinned, oblivious that only empty seats in the cafeteria surrounded them.

* * * * *

"Did you think I wouldn't find you?"

I recognized the dainty voice before I rounded the last corner near the locker. The last bell had already rung, but Mom was in a meeting that would last at least fifteen more minutes. Luckily, she'd decided the boys were finally old enough to walk to the van on their own. Easing around the brick wall, I caught a glimpse of Brianna Lars looming over Rachelle. My friend had backed against the lockers.

"What do you want?" Rachelle asked, her voice pleading.

"For you to hurt. Today, tomorrow, forever." Brianna shoved Rachelle hard against the lockers, in the same way Tosh had pushed me on more than one occasion.

"I'm already hurting," Rachelle said.

"Not enough." Brianna rolled up her sleeves. "You aren't beautiful like Leigh Ann was." She held her pale arm next to Rachelle's face. "She went to the tanning bed religiously, just so her skin would be dark like yours. When I'm finished, everyone will hate you for it."

I had to stop the scene before me. My eyes darted from the books at Rachelle's feet to the lockers that stretched along the vacant hall. What could I move and not give myself away? I thought of Tosh, nearly choking me earlier.

With a good look at the collar that poked out from

beneath Brianna's sweater, I closed my eyes and pictured the white fabric. Slowly, I pulled the two ends closer.

"No one will like the way you look or the way you talk. Rachelle, you'll never be able to look in a mirror again."

I could see the fabric meeting, one corner touching the other. Tighter. Squeezing my eyes, I pictured the white fabric closing around Brianna's neck.

A squeal echoed through the hall. "I can't breathe," Brianna said, running for the nearby doors.

I released Brianna and walked to Rachelle. "Are you okay?"

She blinked, her face full of fury. "You were spying again?"

"No," I said. "Okay, maybe I was."

Rachelle pushed me aside. "Brianna doesn't like me. I told you to stay out of this."

"You can't let her keep threatening you like this."

"You mean like how you let Tosh threaten you for nearly a whole semester?"

I opened my mouth but couldn't think of a good reply. She was right.

"That's what I thought," Rachelle said as she left me standing at the locker.

* * * * *

"What's wrong?" Mom asked that night at dinner.

I looked up from my plate. The steam had faded, but the chicken and rice sat, lumped in the same pile as when Mom spooned it from the pot. "Why does something always have to be wrong?"

Mom chuckled. "Anytime you're not eating

something is definitely wrong."

"There's a new girl at school, Brianna Lars."

"Yes," she said. "I have Brianna for fourth block. She's one of the smartest students I've ever taught. And I couldn't ask for better manners."

"Way to go Jes." Dad patted me on the arm. "Glad to see you're finally making new friends."

"Trust me Dad, Brianna is not who you want me hanging out with."

He straightened. "And why not?"

"She hates Rachelle."

Mom raised her eyebrows. "Brianna Lars?" She laughed. "That girl is harmless. Did you know she volunteers at the hospital? Charlie says Brianna has a real gift for helping people."

Yeah, for helping piss them off. "I didn't think you'd understand."

Mom and Dad exchanged a glance. I took a bite of chicken, which tasted surprisingly good. Pushing my plate away, I laid the fork on the table and leaned back in my chair. "I think I'm done."

Dad stared at me. "You need to eat. You're starting to worry us again."

"Really?" I asked and stood.

"Jes," Dad said, "if there's something on your mind, tell us. If Brianna Lars is such a bad person, then tell us why. Don't shut us out this time."

The only thing I had time for was an extended stay in my room. I turned for the door but couldn't leave the room. Instead, I lowered myself back into the chair. "Brianna is being mean to Rachelle and I'm not sure why."

"Mean like Tosh treated you last year?" Mom asked.

Stop, I told myself. The chills along my spine insisted we were speeding head-first into a dangerous place, a conversation we should never have. "Worse."

"This is serious," Dad said. "Is Brianna physically hurting Rachelle?"

"She hasn't beat her up, not yet. But I'm not sure how much longer that will be."

Mom's face turned to stone. "Has she hurt you?"

"No," I said. "I've tried to stay out of it, but I don't know how long I can watch her call Rachelle those horrible names and threaten her."

Mom gave a nod. "I'll talk with Joel."

I shook my head. "Telling Dr. Greene won't fix this."

"Then what?" Dad asked. "You can't tell us someone is hurting Rachelle and expect us to keep quiet. Something must be done."

"I'll find a way," I said.

"You won't fight her," Dad said.

Mom waved her hand to calm him. "What exactly is Brianna saying?"

"She doesn't like the way Rachelle talks or the color of her skin."

Dad smiled, but it wasn't a happy smile. "You've met people like that before, in the other towns. Sometimes people just hate without understanding why. Hate breeds hate—we've had this discussion before."

"But this is more," I said. "I just haven't figured Brianna out yet." Or Rachelle.

"There isn't always a reason," Dad said. "Remember that girl near Phoenix? She hated you because your skin wasn't as dark as hers."

"It's not like I could ever get a tan with all that

sunscreen you always made me wear."

"That's not the point," Mom said. "People will find a reason to hate if they want to."

"You need to understand," Dad said. "This lesson is important."

"Yeah," I said, "I get it. Don't hate."

Dad frowned. "Don't patronize me. You weren't raised to hate anyone, but you need to accept that some people will never stop."

"This is why I don't tell you guys stuff. I'm worried about Rachelle and you're trying to teach me a stupid lesson."

Mom chuckled again. "What your father is trying to say is that to deal with Brianna you need to first understand why she feels that way."

"I don't care what she feels. I'm not even sure yet if she *does* feel."

"Okay," Dad said. "Let's try this a different way. Danny and Collin are twins, right? Different from you since you have no twin?"

I wanted to laugh. Maybe even cry. "Right."

"This isn't a conversation I want to have," Mom said gruffly.

"But it's one she might understand." He looked at me. "What if we lived in a world where almost everyone had a twin? How would you feel?"

World of twins? He must be really desperate to prove his point. "Different, I guess."

"So," Mom said, "what if Danny and Collin were treated normal and you were treated... different?"

"It wouldn't be fair," I said. "But no one would hate for such a dumb reason."

"Maybe dumb to you," Dad said, "but what if you

did have a twin? What if we *all* had twins? What if your mom and I raised you to hate anyone without a twin? What if I reminded you of this every time we passed one of those people on the street? What if we told you bedtime stories about how bad they are?"

"You'd be wrong," I said. "And it would still sound dumb."

"Of course," Mom said, "that's how you feel now. But years ago…"

I shrugged. It seemed strange, but maybe if they had insisted. "Maybe I would have listened to you."

"What if it wasn't just us?" Dad asked. "What if the whole world thought the same way? What if the government forced people without a twin to live separately, without the same rights? What if your entire career was chosen for you, based on a single test?"

I took a sip of my tea, considering. "I'd have bigger problems than Brianna Lars."

Dad grinned, proud of himself. "See what a little perspective gets you?"

Leaning back in my chair, I made up my mind. "Can I fight back then?"

"Fighting is not the answer," Dad said.

Maybe it was time to turn his lesson against him. "What if I didn't like your fantasy world and decided to change it?"

"Standing in line is always safer," Mom said.

"But it's my life," I said. "Are you saying you'd live your entire life and never fight to make it your own?"

Mom looked at Dad and sighed. "No."

"What kind of government would make this law?"

"The king and queen kind," Dad said.

"Then that's your problem," I said. "Your world

needs an election—representatives of the people, by the people, for the people. Am I the only one here who's had to sit through history class?"

Mom and Dad both stared, amazement in their eyes. "Jessica Ray," he said. "I had no idea you'd developed an interest in government."

I rolled my eyes. "Required reading, duh. But apply it to your world. I'm not suggesting we go Marie Antoinette on them, but get rid of the king and queen. Elect officials. Show people they can all live together."

"You make it sound so easy," Mom said, "like you've got everything figured out."

"Well," I said, "quit acting like it's weird that I think about stuff. You guys have never hesitated to tell me what's right and what's wrong."

Dad nodded. "Agreed. But one day you'll have to remember what we've *stuffed* in your head all these years and figure out how to make good decisions."

Well, at least one good decision had become clear.

I'd continue to use my power to fight Brianna, and no one would ever know.

CHAPTER SEVEN

Bloody Hands

The next morning, Joe was back in class, hunched over the black binder. As his fingers flowed across the page, I thought of the day Bailey and I discovered Chase's binder in Mrs. Pearson's class. I'd never mentioned finding the binder to Chase, and Bailey obviously had never brought it up. He probably had no idea I knew about the binder he used to search for the missing girl.

The name *Jessica Delaney* had hidden quietly within the list of names he'd marked out. Maybe he hadn't been sure about me from the first day we met, like he'd claimed on our last night together. Maybe he had doubts for his entire stay in Credence. After all, the secrets from my past had fooled even me.

I eased into the seat next to him. "What's your last name?"

He stopped writing and looked at me, uncertainty in his face. "Why do you ask?"

"Since Mrs. Austen doesn't take roll, I don't know your last name."

"It's not important."

"To me it is."

"Shh," he said, glancing around. When Joe spoke again, his voice held not a hint of Chase's trademark confidence. "We shouldn't be talking."

I looked around the room. Most of the desks were full, but our teacher had yet to make an entrance. Most people were laughing. A girl to my left chatted about the jerk who refused to play football, even when Credence needed him. No one bothered to look our way.

"This isn't what you think," he said.

"You mean you really aren't here to take me back?"

Joe turned away, refusing to let me see his eyes. "Why would I take you anywhere?"

The mixture of pain and resolution in his voice felt like a smack to my face. Was he teasing me? Would he torture me for refusing to return with him? I reached for Joe's arm.

"Don't do that," he said, pulling back as far as the desk would allow.

"What?" I reached again for his arm. "Get in your personal space?"

"Don't touch me." This time his voice held fear. "Maybe you should find another desk."

I should have told him the same. Instead, I grabbed my backpack and found an empty desk across the room. Tears burned in the corners of my eyes, but not from anger. His refusal to acknowledge the truth had actually hurt, when I thought I'd mastered hiding my feelings from everyone. Guess I couldn't hide them from Chase. Or Joe. Whoever.

What was it with guys not being able to make up their minds? Half the time Pade didn't seem sure if he felt love or hate when I walked into the room. Now Joe had shut me out.

Even worse, a nagging thought had hijacked my brain. What if I really wasn't the girl Chase had been looking for?

* * * * *

"I'm going to the store," Mom said, about an hour after we got home that afternoon.

I looked up from the kitchen table, which was filled with my homework. "Now?"

"Fifteen minutes," Mom said as she planted a kiss on my head. "We're out of milk, and I can't make mashed potatoes without it."

"Are you taking the boys?" I asked.

"They can stay outside with their bikes. Your father will be home any minute."

I rolled my eyes.

"You'll be fine." She grabbed her purse. "I've got my cell phone if you need anything."

"Sure," I said, knowing I couldn't call even if I wanted to. The phone they'd given me back in January, the awesome birthday present I'd never asked for, still sat in its box in my top dresser drawer. Fat chance of it still having enough charge to power up.

Math was done. English, but not history. No thinking about that class tonight. I listened as the van cranked up and pulled out of the driveway. Joe's words still haunted me. I closed my eyes, trying to shut them out. Maybe I wasn't her. I opened my eyes and stared at the spotless floor. We'd lived in Credence for a full year now, which broke our previous record of nine months in Atlanta.

Thankfully, no one had mentioned moving again.

"Jes," yelled Danny from the doorway. "Collin fell off his bike."

I leapt from the chair and shoved myself through the door, trailing behind Danny. My heart hammered against my chest as I slid along the rocks. Collin lay across the pavement at the end of our driveway, not moving. I made it to his side, landing on my knees.

Danny talked so fast I couldn't understand his words. His hands shook nervously as he gripped the sides of his face.

"His leg," I finally understood, about the time I noticed the blood.

Sliding Collin's ripped jeans aside, I surveyed the jagged cut below his hip. My fingers touched the blood and Danny moaned in agony.

"We've got to put pressure on the wound," I heard myself say. When had I learned that?

"Will he be okay?" Danny asked, close to tears.

"Yes," I said, placing my hands against the wound, which gushed blood like water from a fire hose. Sticky red warmth covered my hands and then my arms and legs. I pushed the hair out of my eyes and tried to seal the wound again, with only my hands.

"Get help," I screamed. "Next door."

Danny jumped up and ran toward Bailey's house.

I watched as the blood splattered across the pavement and soaked into the knees of my jeans. Tears stung in my eyes, for the single moment seemed more like an entire movie. I'd been here before. Another time, a place from my dreams. Yes, my hands were sticky then too. Images flashed in my head, first like fireworks exploding in the sky, and then crawling to a stop as if time stood still. A man laid across the dirt before me, my hands pressed against his chest. Blood seeped from the spot where the bullet had entered.

Tears blurred my eyes. It was happening all over again. We were outside—no, wooden rafters filled the space above. The man's arms dropped helplessly at his side. His chest rose and fell for the last time. I was five years old, but even then I knew what happened when a book reached the last page.

I cried for him, the man who'd saved my life. But I couldn't stare at his face or meet the eyes of my father. He was gone. He'd died saving me. Nothing could bring him back.

Climbing to my feet, I ran. Voices yelled behind me, a shuffle of feet trying to grab the gun, rushing to stop me. Forcing myself through a wooden door, I bounded into the snow. My feet were bare, cold as the ice that crackled beneath me, but I couldn't stop. The voices faded as I ran ahead, shoving aside branches that clawed at my face in the darkness.

All was lost. My family was gone. I was on another planet, a million miles from home. A ball of light hung in the night sky, dimmer than a sun but glowing with a sense of belonging, as if an unseen face watched over me. But I was alone. I'd probably die in the lonely woods surrounding me, eaten by whatever hungry animals hid among the brush, or shot by the evil man. His eyes burned, tortured my thoughts, even when I closed mine. My mother and brother would never know what happened to me.

I'd never see them again.

A light flashed in my eyes and I froze. The roar of

an engine came at me, like no spaceship I'd ever heard. Screeching sounds pierced the air and then metal bars stopped only inches from my nose. A door opened as the engine chugged and heaved in my ears. Heat flowed from between the metal bars, melting tears that had frozen to my cheeks. A man stepped into the light, reaching down to me and then a voice called my name.

"Jes."

I fought against the arms around me, aching to wipe the tears from my eyes.

"Easy," the voice said.

Pulling back ever so slightly, I looked up into Pade's eyes. His were filled with an emotion I couldn't name. His arms held me tenderly as his hands smoothed the hair that had finally grown long enough to hang halfway down my back. He placed a light kiss on my forehead, but I didn't have the strength to pull away.

"Are you okay?" he asked.

I burst into laughter at the sound of those words again, but in the next moment tears formed a river down my cheeks.

Pade released me from the circle of his arms, watching intently. He scooted next to me, leaning close enough for me to lay my head against his shoulder. Wrapping his arm around my shoulders, we sat in silence as I cried.

When I finally caught my breath without sobbing, I looked at the empty street before us. "Where is Collin?" Had I imagined the whole episode? I scanned the pavement, sighing when I noticed the blood, dried on the asphalt. I wasn't crazy, but Collin was still hurt.

"Your dad came back and took Collin to the hospital. My mom still had an hour left on her shift.

When I called Uncle Justin, he was only a few miles away."

"Dad… left me… here?"

"Aunt Rainey's going to meet them. You freaked out or spaced out, I'm not sure. You were hysterical."

"Danny?"

"He went too. Look," Pade said and pulled me close, "your dad said Collin will be fine. He couldn't help you both."

Damn, I sounded like a lost puppy. "You stayed with me?"

Pade smiled, sad but sure as he squeezed my shoulders. "There's no place I'd rather be."

* * * * *

That night, I imagined the blue shoe box and it appeared on my dresser. After looking for so many months, I found it hard to believe the dusty box was finally sitting in front of me. I could read every page, twice if I wanted. I understood what Mom had been thinking. She'd hid the box in Aunt Charlie's shed, sure I'd never find it under a foot of dust on the top shelf.

But nothing in that box was mine. It wasn't my past—I was sure now. The man with the gun hadn't stood in any house. We'd been hidden away in thick woods, miles from anything resembling the sandwiched house the Naples stood in front of in the picture, when Marsha Naples had cried, begging for the return of her kidnapped daughter. The sidewalk I supposedly ran down to escape… what a horrible lie.

As I sat on the bed, staring at the box, I realized opening that lid again would be a waste. I wasn't Jessica

Naples. It was time to put New York behind me.

I waved my hand and sent the box back to its lonely shelf.

* * * * *

"Are you sure you're good?" Bailey asked as I finished the last of my pizza.

I nodded and drank my tea. My thirty minutes for lunch was over, but I wasn't in any hurry to get to math class. Not when my mom was the teacher.

Pade sat down next to me. "How many times have you been late to Aunt Rainey's class?"

"More than four," I said.

"She won't write you up," Bailey said.

"Isn't that a conflict of interest?" Tosh asked as she took one of the seats next to Bailey.

I couldn't help but grin. Something about this new, reformed Tosh kept me guessing what she'd say next. "I think the computer putting me in her class was a conflict of interest."

Tosh shrugged. "Your mom helped me last year. I was failing math before her class. I guess you could say the computer is responsible for that too."

Although I would never admit it, she did have a point. I turned to Pade. "I bet Mom never had a problem when you missed her class."

He laughed. "I'd never miss math class. Aunt Rainey might not be the best cook, but she is the best math teacher I've ever known."

"Hey," Bailey said as I grabbed my backpack. "Don't forget about the sleepover at Angel's."

Forget? I'd argued with Dad about Friday for the

last two weeks. "It's conditional."

Bailey raised an eyebrow.

I reached in my purse and pulled out my cell phone.

Shaking her head, Bailey took the phone from my hand. "This phone has been in your dresser for the last six months. It can't still work."

"That kind of battery doesn't go bad in six months," Pade said.

"Whatever." She handed back the phone.

"I just hope we get to fish off Angel's dock." I dropped the phone in my purse and stood. "I really should go. Mom's been on edge after what happened with Collin."

"But he's fine, right?" Tosh asked.

Now Tosh was worried about my family? Unbelievable. "Twelve stitches," I said. "He acts like it's thirty. Dad stayed home with him today, but Mom's hands were still shaking as she cranked the van this morning." Before Tosh could ask anything more, I left the table.

Bailey grabbed my arm at the doors. "I invited Tosh to the party. Is that okay?"

So, now Bailey and Tosh were hanging out? "Would it matter if I cared?"

"Yes," she said, biting her lip. "You're still my best friend."

"Tosh hit me, she made fun of me in front of everyone, and she tried to take Pade. Don't forget how she and Lisa set me up to get busted for skipping." And Lisa had paid the ultimate price.

"I know, but Tosh has changed. She said you started it when you told her to turn in her step-dad, last year at the movies. If only she'd listened to you."

Tosh had told Bailey? "I hated her. I can't just turn it off, like nothing happened between us."

"I understand if you can't forgive her, but will you still come to the party?"

"Yes." I pushed through the doors.

Tosh didn't deserve Bailey's friendship. Bailey asked about me forgiving Tosh, but how could *she* forgive so easily?

I slowed to a walk as the late bell rang. Good thing Mom hadn't written me up yet. She hadn't mentioned my being late so many times, but I had a feeling that discussion loomed on our horizon.

"Jessica Delaney."

My feet froze as I focused on Ronald Pitts. He leaned against the wall next to the fire alarm he'd pulled, sipping from the straw of the clear plastic cup in his hand, which was filled with a blue liquid.

"Can't make it to class on time?" he asked.

"Looks like I'm not the only one," I said.

He smiled, his voice deadly. "Heard you can't keep your mouth shut either."

"I… I don't know what you're talking about."

"Can't lie well either." He took another sip and walked toward me.

Running was my best option, but my feet wouldn't move. I could only watch as he approached.

Ronald removed the lid from his cup. "Did you know Dr. Greene suspended me for three days?"

"Yes."

"It was just a stupid dare to get someone out of class. I can't believe that man suspended me." He looked up and down the hall. "You're going to regret turning me in."

I swallowed, unable to breathe as he raised the cup. "Tell me how sorry you are."

"I'm sorry," I whispered.

"Such a bad liar. Make me believe it."

Glancing up and down the empty hall, I shuddered. No witnesses for whatever he planned. "I'm sorry," I said louder.

"Not good enough." He launched the contents of his cup.

No, I thought and squeezed my eyes shut, preparing for a cold shock, but seconds passed as the sugared water failed to splash against my skin. Opening my eyes, I gasped at the sight before me.

Every molecule of blue liquid hung in the air between us. Like paint splattered on a canvas, the drink seemed to have a solid texture, exploding in all directions, while moving in none. Ronald stared at the liquid, his eyes huge. The cup fell from his hand, crashing to the floor near his feet. His mouth gaped open.

I touched a drop about the size of a dime, with a similar thickness and shape. My finger made a slight dent as the blue disk compressed, like a piece of gummy candy. I pressed harder and the disk moved. Without warning, the blue mass lost its solid form and rained onto the floor around my feet.

"What the hell was that?" Ronald asked, staring at me.

My power. I'd stopped the drink on impulse, not thinking of consequences. A primitive response to danger, but how could I explain? Fear gripped me as I realized Ronald knew my secret.

To my surprise, Ronald grabbed for my arm. "You

really are a freak!"

"I wouldn't do that," said a low voice behind me.

I spun and almost bumped into Joe.

He took a step back, far enough that I couldn't touch him, all the while his eyes stayed fixed on Ronald. "I've heard enough from you."

"You did that?" Ronald asked.

"Yeah," Joe said. "Imagine what else I could do."

Ronald considered. "Shit on that." He took off down the hall.

Joe looked over me. "You shouldn't have done that. Why didn't you just tell him it wasn't you?"

I covered my face with my hands. "I tried, but I'm the worst liar, remember?"

"You're far better than you realize."

"What?" I asked, uncovering my face, but the hall was empty.

* * * * *

"I'm not sure if you staying out tonight is a good idea," Dad said at breakfast on Friday morning.

I took a spoonful of my cereal, still not sure if Dad would okay the party. "It's Angel's birthday. I didn't get to go last year."

Dad chuckled. "You never asked to go last year."

"Because you freaked out about the water on our first day in Credence."

"How was I supposed to feel?" he asked. "You weren't exactly truthful with us."

"Because you two are control freaks."

"We want to keep you safe," he said.

I shook my head and shoved another bite of cereal

into my mouth.

Mom patted Dad's arm. "You didn't win this conversation at fifteen and you're not faring any better at sixteen."

Almost seventeen, I thought. September had already begun, and October fourteenth wouldn't be far. I wondered if they planned to celebrate my birthday on time this year or wait until January. Probably neither since they'd never been much for celebrating birthdays in the past.

"Honey," Mom said, "all we want is for you to be honest with us. You nearly died because you were too afraid to tell us the truth about your illness. How do you think that makes *me* feel?"

"Horrible," I said, dropping the spoon.

"Try worse than horrible," Dad said. "We've all been through a mountain of stress this week. A *quiet* weekend is the ticket. Besides, I want us to sit down and discuss what happened with you when Collin was hurt."

I looked down at my hands, still feeling the warm blood as if the smear of red had been tattooed across my skin.

"You remembered something." Dad's eyes held the same look from the morning I confronted him about the Naples, who'd turned out to be a lie to keep me safe. "I want us to talk about this as a family. We've always known you faced a trauma, and I think you've finally begun to remember what happened the night I found you."

Tears welled in my eyes. "I tried to help Collin. I'm sorry I lost it."

Dad pushed back his chair and put an arm around me. "I'm sorry I had to leave you like that."

I leaned against him and cried into his chest.

He circled his other arm around me. "I didn't have a choice. Pade was there and I know you don't exactly like him, but…"

I raised my head. He still thought I didn't like Pade? "It was the blood—I remembered blood on my hands and then… I… I blacked out."

Mom's voice was sad. "Whose blood?"

My real father's. "I'm not sure."

Dad put a hand on my cheek. "It's important that you remember." His voice lowered to a whisper. "Time is running out, Kay Ray. I need you to remember."

I stared at his face. Sounds flashed in my head, a few words, maybe only a feeling, before the memory passed and I was back in Credence.

"Still not sure?" Dad asked. "Your eyes tell a different story."

I couldn't breathe, not with the strange look on his face. Pushing his arms away, I stood. "I've told you all I know. What else do you want from me?"

Dad backed away, pain glimmering in his eyes. Without another word, he turned and headed for the porch.

"Guess you won," Mom said, after the door slammed. "We'll talk tomorrow when you come back from the party."

I forced a smile. If I'd really won the battle, why did I feel so low?

* * * * *

"What should we drink tonight?" Angel asked.

"Tequila," Bailey said. "I want the worm."

Angel nodded and opened the globe that filled an entire corner of her living room. It was her parent's liquor cabinet, a piece of furniture passed down from Angel's grandmother. Angel's mother often forgot to lock it when they were away. Rachelle sat next to me on the couch but didn't bother looking up from her phone. Tosh stood near the door, as if she might bolt from the party at any moment.

A knock sounded and Angel slammed the globe, running for the door. "Act normal," she said, before opening the door.

"Everything okay in here?" A woman with glasses peaked through the screen. "Any boys tonight?"

Angel grinned. "Just us girls, Señora Giménez."

"Bueno, mis niñas. I'll return to check on you later."

"We look forward to it," Angel said. When the door closed, she sighed. "My parents go out of town and claim they trust me, but then send the neighbor. How's that for trust?"

Bailey rolled her eyes and looked at me. "Can we get on with this?"

Another knock sounded on the door. "What now?" Angel asked and swung open the door.

Pade stood on the steps. "Hey."

Angel's forehead creased. "What are you doing here?"

He held out a white container with a lid. "Jes mentioned wanting to fish tonight, so I got some bait."

"Aww," Angel said, clasping her hands together, "isn't that sweet." She turned around. "Jes, you've got a visitor."

"It isn't all like that," Pade said. His cheeks turned a faint shade of red.

I opened the screen door and reached for the container of worms. "Thanks."

"No problem." For a long moment Pade stood, smiling at me. When he turned to leave, I felt a pang in my chest that surprised me.

I'd once thought I loved Pade Sanders, but that crazy high felt nothing like what I felt as he walked to the jeep. I'd wanted him so badly a year ago, but now… now I didn't want to *have* him as much as I wanted to be *near* him. If only I could ditch the party and take a ride in the jeep. He had the top off. My hair would dance in the breeze as the music jammed.

Angel patted me on the back. "I know we all joked about him liking you before, but I think the joke might be on us."

"He's just being Pade," I said.

She laughed. "The old Pade was sweet in his own way, but this new Pade… I'm not so sure about him anymore."

"Oh no," Rachelle said, "Bailey spilled the Tequila."

"Bailey!" Angel yelled and rushed to grab the bottle.

"I didn't spill anything," Bailey said.

"I saw it fall," Rachelle insisted. "You'll never get that smell out of the carpet."

I knelt next to Bailey and ran a hand over the carpet. "It feels dry to me."

"See," Bailey said.

Rachelle shook her head. "I could have sworn."

"Next time don't," Bailey said.

"Sorry," Rachelle said, but the word held an edge of anger.

"Enough," Angel said. "Since Pade was so sweet, let's go fishing."

We each picked from a bundle of poles that leaned against the back porch and chose a canvas chair from a stack nearby. I pulled my chair out of the bag as we reached the end of Angel's dock. The sun was disappearing fast behind the trees across the river, leaving flares of orange and red to bounce from cloud to cloud. The water slept before us, with not a single boat in sight to shatter the glass surface. The air felt cool, but no one wore a jacket. It was enough that summer had finally begun to fade.

I cast my line, smiling as it broke the surface, but the single splash and outward waves quickly calmed back to glass. A fish jumped about ten feet from the dock, taunting us, and Angel pointed with a laugh. Life was perfect.

Everyone had a drink, except for Tosh, though I barely finished half of mine. Even though I only had half of a shot-glass in the cup, I made a mental note that tequila would never be a drink of choice for me. Only Rachelle caught a fish, but we stayed on the dock long after the stars appeared. The moon glowed, a larger-than-life ball of fire that Angel referred to as a 'harvest' moon.

The happiness faded when Angel brought up Skip. "His birthday is next Saturday."

"Oh yeah?" Bailey asked, but I could tell she didn't want to talk about Skip.

"I've decided on his birthday present." Angel cleared her throat. "I'm going to give it to him."

Rachelle's smile died.

Bailey choked on her drink, spitting a mouthful over the dock's edge. "You mean your virginity?"

Tosh spoke for the first time that night. "Oh, no."

"Skip will be eighteen," Angel said softly. "I'm seventeen now. We've been dating for almost a year." She gripped the sides of her chair. "I want him to know how I feel."

Bailey stood. "Guys are idiots." She dumped the remains of her drink into the water. "He'll just leave you."

Angel shook her head. "Skip will never leave."

"Keep believing that." Turning toward the house, Bailey stomped until her feet reached the dirt.

The dock began to drift up and down in waves.

"What did you do?" Angel yelled. "Give it up to Chase before he left?"

Bailey stopped. "Don't ever say that again." The force of her words shocked me, or maybe it was how her voice sounded so close to tears.

I ran after Bailey, following her into the house, and found her sitting on the bathroom floor, gripping her knees. Tears poured down her cheeks.

"Hey," I said, grabbing her arms. "It's okay."

"Chase is never coming back," she wailed. "You aren't the girl, remember?"

It was the perfect moment to tell Bailey about my memories. I could share my suspicions about Joe, and she could help me discover the truth. It made perfect sense—she knew the truth about New York, about Lauren, and even the fact that Chase was from outer space. But I couldn't say the words. No way would I put her through losing Chase again. "Right."

She sniffled. "I thought I could move on and forget about him."

"Bailey, you and Chase didn't…"

"Yeah, right. I'm about as slutty as you could ever

be." She smiled through the tears. "If only I could see him again."

Angel knocked on the bathroom door. "I've got something to show you guys. We'll be in the living room."

Bailey wiped the tears. "Let's get back to tonight."

In the living room, Angel stood holding a box. "Mom got this for my birthday."

"Oh my god," Bailey said. "Where did she find this?"

The box seemed to be a game. The picture showed a board with letters and numbers, almost like a paper keyboard, but arranged in sequence. A beige heart-shaped piece of plastic with a clear circle at its center sat below the word Ouija.

"What is it?" I asked.

"You've never seen a Ouija board?" Rachelle asked. "They're super cool."

"I've always wanted one," Bailey said, taking the box.

Was I the only one who'd never played this game? I looked at Tosh, who stared at the box. "I want to play first," she said.

Bailey laughed. "We all play this together." She turned to me. "It's supposed to be like a psychic experience. We all touch the planchette at the same time. If there's a spirit in the room, the essence of that person guides us to move across the letters, spelling a message."

"Ghosts?" I asked, stunned. I'd read stories but nothing had ever happened to make me believe in ghosts.

"It's silly," Rachelle said. "The chances of ghosts being real rank right up there with flying saucers, but it should be fun."

"Flying saucers?" Bailey asked while nudging my arm.

I sighed. "Okay. Is the ghost supposed to be haunting Angel's house?"

"We can use this to contact someone on the other side," Tosh said. "We can talk to Lisa."

Angel's face looked uncertain as she considered. "What will it hurt?" she finally asked.

We formed a circle on the wooden section of the living room floor as Angel lit three candles and turned off the lights. She placed the candles in a triangle around us.

"Shouldn't you make a star?" Rachelle asked.

"Mom only had three candles," Angel said.

"Are you scared?" Bailey whispered to me.

"Not at all," I said.

Tosh stared at the board intently, closing her eyes as we all placed a hand on the planchette, as Bailey had called it. I shrugged to Bailey and closed my eyes.

"Lisa," Angel said, "if you're here, talk to us."

The room pulsed with an almost electric feeling, though it was eerily silent. A loud click sounded and we jumped.

"That's just the air turning on," Angel said.

My heart raced, but I wasn't sure why. Could Lisa really be near? I settled a hand on the heart-shaped game piece once again, along with everyone else. Again, Angel called to Lisa, and again the room was silent like a movie from a hundred years ago.

"This is so fake," Rachelle said.

I grinned, thinking about how I could move the plastic with my mind, if I only focused.

The planchette broke from my hand.

Rachelle screamed.

I opened my eyes to see Rachelle dancing around, gripping her knee. "It hit me! Who did that?"

Looking around, I watched each person in the circle. Tosh was stunned. Angel looked fearful. Bailey… stared at the lifeless piece of plastic.

Rachelle pointed at Bailey. "You made it hit me."

"How?" Bailey asked. "First you accuse me of dropping the tequila. Now I hit you?"

Angel raised her hands. "Stop it, you two."

Was my power getting stronger? I'd stopped Ronald's drink. I'd thought about moving the planchette. Had I?

Rachelle went back to her knees. "If it didn't happen, how did this piece of junk get to my leg?"

Bailey shrugged. "Maybe it was Jes or Angel."

"Maybe it was Lisa," Tosh said.

"No," Rachelle said. "Too many weird things have been happening lately, and Bailey is always there."

"How?" Bailey asked again.

Tosh pushed the board away. "Maybe you thought about it and made it happen like telekinesis." She looked at me. "I've studied several cases in the last few months that seem to prove it's possible."

Bailey looked at me, a clear question in her eyes. I'd never told her about the day Chase opened all the lockers and sent Tosh running for the doors.

Yes, Chase. Maybe he wasn't just watching over me. Had he shown himself to Bailey, or was he close enough to make 'weird things' happen? Would she be so upset about Chase being gone if she knew he'd returned?

"Okay," Bailey said, "maybe I did push it at your

leg. I'm sorry."

"That's so not cool." Tosh stood. "I think I'm ready for bed."

"I'm sorry you guys," Bailey said. "It was just a joke."

Angel frowned. "I can't believe you made fun of Lisa."

Bailey hung her head, but she never mentioned Chase again that night.

CHAPTER EIGHT

Reality Check

"Have fun?" Pade asked when he picked us up the next morning.

"Not really," Bailey said, tossing her bag into the jeep. She wasted no time climbing over the side and buckling herself in the backseat.

"What happened?" he asked.

"Silly girl stuff," I said.

He looked concerned. "Did Tosh cause problems? Did she say anything to upset you?"

I climbed into the passenger seat. "She barely said anything all night."

"Can we get out of here today?" Bailey asked.

"Sure." Pade cranked the jeep.

We sped down the dirt road, sliding a few times as he moved too close to the road's edge. Each time Pade recovered with a laugh, but Bailey refused to smile. He cranked up the radio. I fought my hair as it caught in my eyes. A truck passed us and Pade slammed the gas, catapulting us through the oncoming cloud of dust.

As we pulled onto the pavement, Pade glanced at me. "Want to go out tonight?"

"Yeah," I said, but pounded my knee when I remembered Dad's words from the night before.

Pade turned down the music. "Other plans?"

"Dad wants to talk about what happened the night Collin got hurt."

"Have you remembered what happened?" he asked.

"Not yet."

"Well, if your schedule opens up, I thought we might go to the movies. Skip's taking Angel and he mentioned maybe you and I could come."

"That sounds awesome." Two hours of nothing but eating popcorn and drowning myself in a world of action and adventure. I could hold Pade's hand. But Dad had insisted on a family session.

Bailey grumbled. "Does that mean I've got to go too? Are you guys still going to keep up the 'friends' cover?"

I nodded. "My parents can't know. They already think I'm mental."

Bailey stuck her head between us. "No one thinks that."

"We'll see after today, after we all 'talk' about my past."

"What if you do remember?" Pade asked. "What then? Back to the blue box?"

I considered the fact I hadn't looked through the box again. After all, it wasn't really my past. If only I could tell them the truth.

* * * * *

"In here," Mom said, from the living room.

I dropped my bag in the hall and took the spot next to her on the couch. I crossed my legs and drew a long breath. Closing my eyes, I prepared for the speech.

"Your father had to leave," she said.

My eyes shot open. "Leave?" I looked around the room. "To where?"

Mom took my hand in hers. "Back to the hospital in Atlanta."

"Are you kidding me?"

"He hasn't been feeling… himself lately. Dr. Baynor called in some tests, just to be sure."

"Sure of what? Has his cancer returned?"

The ensuing silence felt as if someone had built an invisible box around me. I couldn't seem to move from my space on the couch.

"I don't think so." Mom squeezed my hand. "He had blood work done when you were in Atlanta, and everything looked good. It's merely a precaution."

"Then why is your hand shaking?"

She pulled away. "I didn't want to upset you. Truth is, this week has been too much for me. The boys wanted to stay the night with Sam and I didn't argue. It's a relief they've gotten close to Joel's youngest son. They haven't mentioned any friends from Atlanta lately."

I sighed, thankful they were gone. Hopefully Skip didn't mention going out to his brother. "Can we skip the family meeting until Dad comes home?"

"Sure," she said. "We could have a quiet evening."

I opened my mouth, already feeling guilty. "Bailey wants to go to the movies. Pade is going to drive us."

"You've seen a lot of Pade this week."

"He's Bailey's brother."

"Yes, I know." She took my hand again. "Charlie and I worried last year—every time Pade was near, you seemed to get upset. Your father and I had several discussions about the two of you, trying to figure out how you could hate Pade so much. You barely knew him growing up."

"I don't hate Pade."

"Are you sure?"

I nodded and squeezed her hand back. "Mom?"

"Yes?"

"Don't tell Dad—but if I ever did realize I sort of like Pade, or maybe really like Pade, not that I do, but if I did at some crazy point in the future, would you freak out?"

Mom smiled. "Don't tell your father—but would you freak out if I said no?"

I hugged her, for I had the best mom in the world.

* * * * *

"What do you think about skipping the movies?" Pade asked as I reached the jeep.

"But you said—"

"We could hang out, just you and me."

"What about Angel and Skip?"

Pade glared at the front door of his house. "Bailey isn't in any hurry tonight."

"I didn't ask about Bailey."

He frowned and turned back to me. "They went swimming at the river."

"Alone?"

"We were invited, but… I didn't think us going would be a good idea." Pade squirmed in the driver's seat. "Not after what happened when Collin—"

"Because I freaked out? Or is it because of the water?" I asked. "I've told you before. I'm not afraid."

"Do you even know how to swim?"

"I took lessons at one of the other schools. Mom and Dad never knew."

Pade laughed as Bailey locked the door and ran toward the jeep. "Why do we have to hide stupid things from our parents?"

"Please," I begged, leaning close to his face, "it will be fun."

"Promise you're not going to freak out on me?"

"I swear." Maybe I could forget about Dad being back in Atlanta. "The river would be great right now."

Bailey rolled her eyes. "Better bring a change of clothes."

Fifteen minutes later, Pade pulled the jeep into a gas station. Bailey climbed out and stood next to him. "Have fun," she said and ran to a white Pontiac parked next to pump number six.

Tosh stood next to the beat-up car, pumping gas. She waved to us as Bailey reached the passenger door.

"Tosh has a car?"

Pade laughed. "It's her mom's. She and Bailey are going out."

The way he looked at me brought a smile to my face. I touched the collar of my shirt. I'd slipped on the gold necklace Pade gave me all those months ago, for the birthday that wasn't really mine. Although I'd decided against fastening the clasp many times, this night Pade won. Too bad I planned to keep it hidden beneath my shirt, not ready to admit my heart still soared every time he smiled at me.

Pade drove toward Angel's house, but instead of taking her road, he chose a dirt road I'd never noticed. We bounced as the jeep slid around the deep holes. At times the tires spun, bucking us from side to side until I felt sure we'd be stuck. The woods thickened to either side as we passed beyond the area where houses changed from sparse to nonexistent.

The jeep fishtailed as Pade took a corner too fast. I grabbed for the door handle. Pade talked fast, excited about our final stop, still not giving away crucial details. We topped a hill and Pade slammed on the gas, sending us flying ahead so fast I closed my eyes. We could have slammed into a tree or flipped over, but no amount of pleading from me convinced him to slow down.

Just when I thought we'd entered a nightmare, the jeep slowed and came to a stop next to Skip's red truck. Pade killed the engine and for a moment we sat in complete silence. Then I noticed the chirping of crickets. Birds cried in the air, from miles away. Water sloshed at the edge of hearing; we were near the river.

Pade helped me from the jeep. "Wasn't that a rush?"

"Yeah," I said, my heart still racing. "Where are Skip and Angel?"

He pointed to a trail, barely visible in the moonlight. "That way."

Pade climbed the hill ahead of me, talking with no fear of someone hearing. He pawed the briers away, holding the lower ones from my face. The moon stole the night sky, casting a silver hue across the ground. I thought of Chase, a million miles away on a planet with no moon. Or was he in Credence, lying to me? Not sure which was worse, tears filled my eyes. I wiped at the moisture and stumbled through the light, making my way into a gleaming mist that thickened as we approached the water.

"Do I need to walk behind you?" Pade asked.

"No, you should lead the way."

Through the bushes, I saw water to our right—if not for the moon it would have been invisible. The silver glow filled all the gaps between the leaves, which had already begun to fall. I swore as a brier caught my arm. With my power, I could simply push the needle-like thorns away. If only I could keep Pade from noticing.

Pade turned and grabbed my hand. "Be careful. We've still got a long way to go."

Above us the hill seemed to stretch to the sky. Where were we going? My feet were already screaming with the pain of blisters on each toe. Just when I thought the hill would never end, Pade scaled the top and pulled me up behind him.

Beyond our feet were tracks, overgrown rails that led to a bridge, surrounded by a complex structure of metal beams, crisscrossing into the sky.

"Ever heard someone brag about jumping off the train trestle?"

"Yes," I said, filled by awe over how far the weathered metal stretched. As a makeshift roof, several metal bars collided to form a repeating X.

"Don't worry." Pade tugged my arm. "There hasn't been a train on these tracks in years."

Fear rose inside of me with each step. Several of the wooden planks were rotted and barely hanging on. Some of them were missing completely. I shuddered to think with one wrong step we might be in the water.

"Keep your feet on the metal," Pade said.

I eyed the water to either side of the bridge. If I slipped, I could always zap myself somewhere else, if I could only keep my fear in check. But what about Pade? I muffled a laugh with my hand. What would he say? Was my power strong enough to save us both?

"Don't look down," Pade whispered, as water started to show through the boards.

"There they are," a voice yelled.

Up ahead stood Skip and Angel, leaning against a metal beam.

"Watch this," Angel screamed and jumped over the side.

I looked down, nausea overwhelming me at the shear distance between us and the water.

Skip jumped next, as her scream carried across the water, not fading until her feet broke the crystal surface. One set of rings appeared, left by Angel when her body went under, and then another set of rings only feet away, left by Skip. It felt like a set of eyes staring up at me until the water calmed. Skip pushed back through the surface first, followed by Angel.

I released my breath. Seeing Skip and Angel safe slowed my racing heart, but not by much.

"We'll take this slow." Pade pulled me along the bridge.

"Jump, Jes," Angel called from below. The sound echoed up as if bouncing around a canyon. "It's amazing!"

I pulled away from Pade, stepping closer to look over the edge. A cold fear sickened me. *It's not the water*, I told myself. The moonlight faded and I was on that platform again, staring down at Chase.

Pade's lips were moving—I felt the sound even if I

couldn't hear it. I turned as he took my hand.

"I won't let anything happen to you," he said.

My teeth chattered. "What… could… happen?"

"I promise to always be there for you, to protect you no matter what." He pulled me back from the edge and circled his arms around my waist. "We're different—I get that. The secrets you carry from New York make it hard for you to trust me. No matter what happens, don't forget I care about you. I've never stopped loving you."

The intensity in his eyes scared me. I couldn't breathe. My lungs no longer worked. His arms tightened, pulling me close until his lips were on mine.

Somehow, I must have found a breath because the kiss didn't stop. I'd never felt anything like the shock when Pade's tongue touched mine. I wrapped my arms around his neck, taking in the raw smell of his sweat merging with the iron rails. It was everything I'd hoped for, and more emotions than I ever imagined. My stomach swirled until he broke away.

"Wow," Pade said as he stepped back. "Now is the perfect moment."

He held my hands as we climbed through the rails to stand on the outside edge.

"Ready?" he asked.

I took a deep breath. "No."

"On three… one, two, threeeee!"

The water rushed up as we plummeted, leaving no room for more thoughts. For a split second, I could see the stars above us, a perfect dome-shape of light surrounding the moon. Then cold water wrapped around me, holding my body stiff as I dropped below the surface. I opened my eyes, seeing the moon as a hazy silver coin dancing beyond the water. Waving my arms, I kicked my feet and propelled toward the surface. As if bursting through a ceiling of glass, I pushed the last inches of water away and took a huge gulp of air. My lungs begged for more as a thrilling sensation surged through my veins. I was alive and in that moment, nothing in the world mattered more.

Pade laughed from a few feet away. He swam to my side and pulled me close. He kissed me again, pulling me so tight against his chest I felt his heartbeat. Maybe it was faster than mine.

"Get a room," Skip yelled. He and Angel laughed.

Pade released me but held onto my hands. "Have you ever felt a greater high?"

I joined in the laughter, shaking my head. "Never."

If only the feeling would never end.

* * * * *

On the following Thursday, Bailey rushed into the cafeteria, midway through first lunch. "Jes, we need to talk."

I looked up from my tray. "Maybe we should wait until after I finish eating."

"It's about Tosh."

"About time you told her," Rachelle said.

My stomach churned. "Told me what?"

Angel looked away. Bailey tapped her fingers on the table, which matched her nervous voice.

"Tosh is pregnant," Rachelle said. "People are saying the baby is Pade's."

"It's not," Bailey said, slamming her hand on the table. She shoved a finger in Rachelle's face. "Don't ever say that again."

Stunned, I couldn't move. I couldn't speak. No one at the table said anything for what seemed like hours.

"I offered myself to Skip," Angel finally said. "He turned me down."

Rachelle looked at her. "That's… good… I hope."

Angel coughed. "Skip said it wasn't time. He said we should wait until I'm ready."

"That's not good," Bailey said. "That's great!" She looked at me and Rachelle. "Maybe I was wrong. Maybe all guys aren't idiots."

"No," Angel said, "you were right. Guys are idiots."

Bailey held up her hands. "What are you talking about? He totally respected you."

"He said I wasn't old enough yet. He said he wants to go to college and if he gets me pregnant then… well, let's just say it won't fit his plan."

"He made sense," Bailey said. "You took it the wrong way."

"Don't you get it?" Angel grabbed her bag and stood. "He doesn't care about me." She turned to me. "I don't know why you're worried. Pade didn't come back to Credence until August. Tosh's baby can't possibly be his, if she's really pregnant." Pushing through the crowd, Angel headed for the doors.

She was right. I tried to calm my stomach. Pade loved me. He wouldn't mess with Tosh. He was with me in the hospital. We'd talked, he'd helped me recover. He didn't go back to Credence until I did, he… the thought failed as I looked at Rachelle. She sat in silence, staring at the table.

I remembered the call Pade got in July, when he rushed from the hospital to see Tosh.

Bailey watched me. "Did I miss something?"

"He came back to Credence in July," I said. "I overheard him on the phone with Tosh."

"She's right," Rachelle said.

"Look," Bailey said to me, "Pade loves you. Tosh has some drama I can't discuss right now, but it isn't with my brother. You can't possibly think…"

"What if I do?"

Bailey stood. "Then you're not the person I thought."

* * * * *

On Friday morning, a man with twill pants and a blue silk shirt stood before the board in Mrs. Austen's class. He scribbled Mr. Jones and tossed the chalk in the tray. "Didn't think we still had chalkboards," he mumbled as I walked by.

I sat in my usual seat, but no one sat beside me. *Joe has to be here*, I thought as I stared at the black binder. The late bell rang, but still no Joe. About halfway through class, curiosity won and I reached for the binder. I opened to the single page.

Jes, keep this with you always. If you ever find trouble you can't survive, press the stone.

I will return.

Below the words sat a golden K, about the size of a quarter. In the center was a green stone that glimmered no matter how I angled the page, almost pulsing like a heart. I pulled the charm from the page, surprised that no tape or glue held it to the paper. Had Chase left the charm for me? The K must be for Kayden. My fingers tingled as I traced the edges. Excitement welled inside of me.

I put the binder back on Joe's desk. Grinning, I loosened the gold chain around my neck and slid on the charm. Tucking it back under the neck of my shirt, the metal felt cold against my skin. Looking to my side, a sense of loneliness overtook me. The binder was gone.

Rachelle stood by the door after class.

"What's wrong?" she asked. "Looks like you're about to cry."

Okay, time for a distraction. "I just need to see Joe again. He borrowed my… history book." I cringed, for my voice sounded like a lie about a lie.

"Who's Joe?" Rachelle asked as she followed me down the hall.

So much for a distraction. "The guy I've been sitting next to since class started. Well, except for that day I moved across the room."

"I remember—you were talking to yourself. Everyone was whispering because you were… louder than normal."

I turned so fast I nearly tripped. "What do you mean, louder than normal?"

She looked down the hall. "I didn't want to say anything, but you've been talking to yourself since school started. Everyone thinks it's a side effect of your coma."

"Every morning I sit next to Joe…"

Her eyes shifted back to me. "Joe who?"

I thought for a moment. "He never told me his last name, but he's got brown hair and huge arms—maybe he's a wrestler. And his skin is super tan."

She laughed softly. "Jes, you sit at the back of the room, by yourself. You always choose the same desk, but no one sits to either side."

My voice seemed stuck in my throat. "He—he's real. I swear. Joe sits next to me every day."

Rachelle touched my arm. "It's okay if you feel weird sometimes. I asked my mom about it, and she's sure there's nothing wrong with you. Maybe you should tell your parents."

"What about Mrs. Austen? Did I imagine her too?"

"No. She was filling in until Mr. Jones came back from surgery. Didn't you hear what he said when class started?"

My only thoughts had been focused on the binder. "You don't believe me about Joe?"

"Buff guy, dark skin—I bet he's cute."

"Yeah," I said, as my stomach sank.

"Even if he's not my type, I would have noticed a guy sitting next to you."

"I can't believe this," I whispered. Joe had been real. Surely someone had seen him, called his name. I replayed our mornings of silence, along with the few times we talked and seemed to be okay. Mrs. Austen never called his name, and now she was gone. The night Chase and Mrs. Pearson left flashed through my head. Was it happening all over again?

Ronald had seen Joe. Not only seen him but accused him of stopping the drink mid-air in the hall. I could ask Ronald.

No, I couldn't. Ronald had been avoiding me for days. He thought I was a freak.

Maybe he was right.

"Don't worry, Jes," Rachelle said. "I'll keep your secret."

Another secret? Just what I needed.

* * * * *

The stadium was already overflowing by the time Pade pulled into the parking lot, and the only remaining spots were across the street, behind the track. I put on my jacket, despite the fact the September air felt more like July.

Bailey struggled to keep up with Pade. "You shouldn't put yourself through this."

"It's not about me," Pade said. "This is about the team and I want to see Credence win, even if I can't play."

I climbed the steps behind him, still unable to ask about Tosh. Bailey hadn't said a word, but I knew her silence wouldn't last forever. Even though my feet ached after the long walk, I didn't ask to stop. I'd follow Pade all the way to the top if necessary.

Pade stared straight ahead as people jeered. Bailey shook her fist at a guy who tried to trip Pade, but he didn't seem to notice. About three rows from the top, Pade chose an empty row, scooting over for us to sit down.

"We should have gone to the movies," Bailey said, sitting to his other side.

I could feel the anger radiating from my friend. "Like last week?" I asked.

"No one went to the movies last week." Her words weren't playful in the least as she stretched her neck to see the players line up. "Is that the new Q.B.?"

"Brandon Lake," Pade said. "He's a sophomore, but he has potential."

I looked at Pade, stunned. "You've gone to practice?"

"Haven't missed one," he said. "I told you, this isn't about me."

Bailey slapped Pade on the back. "My brother's been teaching Brandon all his secrets."

"Terrance isn't fine with it, but Coach has finally given up on convincing me to play."

Cheers rose as Brandon threw a twenty-yard pass to Terrance, but two plays later Terrance grabbed the ball only to be slammed to the ground. Pade jumped to his feet as two guys from the other team piled on top of Terrance.

"Face mask! That was a hard hit," he said, concern in his eyes, but relaxed when Terrance stood.

"I hope he's okay," I said.

Bailey cheered as Terrance lined up again. "He's always been tough."

Eventually the ball turned over, leaving Credence on defense. Back and forth, the ball zigzagged down the field, more times than I'd been late for Mom's class. Still, no one scored.

With one minute on the clock, Credence lost the ball, leaving a tide of moans across the seats. Closer, the other team made it to the ten-yard line. Surely it would be over soon. If not a touchdown, they'd kick a field goal. I reached for Pade's hand.

Pade squeezed my fingers and put his arm around my neck. The ball was snapped, the quarterback caught it, winding up to pass… but slipped and fell as the ball landed in the hands of a Credence jersey. Our player dodged two hits, gripping the ball as he was shoved out of bounds.

"We've got it," Bailey squealed.

Time was almost gone. In the next play, Brandon threw the ball and it soared down the field, into… Terrance's hands. Terrance had the ball. Terrance was running.

Pade gripped my shoulders. Bailey bounced up and down, screaming. Everyone around us stood as Terrance crossed the line and scored.

"Oh my god," Bailey said, "we won."

"No thanks to Sanders," someone said, but I didn't bother trying to find the voice.

Next to me Pade smiled as if he stood on the field.

* * * * *

That night I left my window open, despite the fact the air was on. The breeze drifting through the screen felt like a sticky summer night, even in September. But I needed heat. The world around me had turned cold. Dad had returned from Atlanta but didn't seem thrilled about how the tests went. And I couldn't stop thinking about Pade.

Turning, I glanced at the clock on my nightstand. Eleven forty-five. I needed to sleep, although time was running out. Tomorrow would be a morning filled with yawns. I'd have to sneak a soda from the fridge before leaving.

A chattering sounded from beyond the window, but I stayed in bed, too lazy to get up and check out what was probably no more than a squirrel on a nearby branch. The chattering came again and then a voice.

I sat straight up. Someone was outside my window. I scrambled from the bed, kneeling in front of the window. A hooded figure moved in the shadows.

"Chase," I whispered, catching my breath. Had he finally decided to come back for me? Happiness surged inside of me, for he was the only one with a reason to sneak around my house.

"Chase," I said against the screen. He didn't seem to notice me as he circled to the front of the house. Was he really going to use the front door?

Easing down the stairs, I nearly crawled until I reached the living room. The carpet was a dark path before me, dotted at the edges with moonlight spilling from the windows. A light darted outside one of the windows, shining a narrow beam near my face. I jumped back into the safety of darkness.

Muffled voices sounded, but instead of the front door, the beacons of light outside seemed to be moving toward the rear of the house. I tiptoed to the kitchen door and carefully pushed it open.

The kitchen was like a dungeon, bathed in darkness. I couldn't make out the bar or the table or even the porch door. It was as if every window in the room had been covered with a blanket. I couldn't see the gaps in the blinds. Light from the moon should be bursting through, forming a ladder of silver lines across the floor.

My racing heart nearly stopped when the door handle clicked. Someone was coming in. I turned, fearful of who might be on the other side. Chase wouldn't use the door—he'd simply zap himself inside. This felt wrong. I closed my eyes, imagining myself back upstairs, but I opened them to the same darkness. How had I made my power work in the woods?

I needed to get out. I backed against the door to the living room. No, it was the wall I felt behind me. I reached along the wall, desperate for my escape. The porch door moved. Footsteps sounded in the kitchen. My eyes barely made out faint light that outlined the door. I opened my mouth but couldn't scream. I needed to wake Mom and Dad.

The light above flipped on and Mom stood in the room's center. Her hair danced wildly around her head and the cotton nightgown almost reached her feet. At five feet and barely one hundred and twenty pounds, I'd never considered her dangerous. But her eyes gleamed with a determination that scared me. Her only focus was the shotgun in her hands and the masked figure who knelt before her.

"Take off the mask. Slowly," she warned as she moved closer.

I held my breath as the mask came off, but it wasn't Chase.

"Who are you?" Mom demanded.

"You know me," the guy squeaked.

"That's not what I mean," she said, shoving the gun at his nose.

"Holy shit—it's me, Ronald Pitts. I'm in your pre-cal class. First block!"

Mom tightened her grip on the gun. "Who are you really?"

Tears spilled from Ronald's eyes as his face twisted in horror. "Ronald. Please don't hurt me."

"Why are you in my kitchen?" Mom asked, her voice deadly.

"It was supposed to be a joke. We were going to scare Jes."

I heard a noise and turned to my left.

Dad stood at the light switch. He put a finger to his lips and moved to Mom's side, placing a hand on her arm. "Lorraine, put the gun down. I think this is one for the police."

"No," Mom said, pressing the gun against Ronald's forehead. "Tell me the truth."

Ronald's voice shook. "Weird things have been happening at school—stuff moving by itself."

Dad looked at me and then back down at Ronald. "Go on," he said.

"She's a freak," Ronald said in agony and covered his face. "Are you all freaks like her?"

"Ronald," Mom said and lowered the gun, "are you on something?"

"No. Maybe." He shook his head. "I don't know what's happening to me. I think I'm going crazy. The doc adjusted my meds, but nothing seems to help."

Mom let out a nervous laugh and took a step back.

"Get up," Dad said. "Call you parents." He turned to me. "Jes, go to the living room."

As I sank into the sofa, I wondered where to begin. What would Dad want to know? What kinds of questions would he ask after seeing Ronald on our kitchen floor?

I watched as the clock passed the ten-minute mark. A car pulled up in front of the house. A knock sounded at the door. To my surprise, Dr. Greene stepped through after Dad opened the door. A woman followed.

Dr. Greene shook Dad's hand. "This is Ronald's mother, Catherine Pitts."

Her hand trembled as Dad closed his around it. "I'm not sure what's going on here, but Ronald and I shall have a *long* talk."

"I'm not sure either," Dad said.

"Joel," Mom said as she crossed the room. "He's in the kitchen crying his eyes out."

"Good," Dr. Greene said. "Thanks for not pressing charges."

Mom looked at the woman close to tears herself. "I'm not sure what's going on between the kids, but it doesn't seem that Ronald planned to hurt anyone. We've all done stupid stuff."

Ronald's mom eyed the gun leaning against the recliner. "Is that loaded?" she asked, her voice shaking.

"Of course," Mom said. She ushered Ronald's mom into the kitchen, with Dr. Greene close behind.

Dad sat on the couch. "Do you have any idea what Ronald was talking about?"

"Last year he picked on me at school. Now he's mad because I turned him in for pulling the fire alarm."

"What about the 'stuff moving by itself'?"

"I don't know, Dad, it sounds like something out of a movie."

He gave me a critical stare. "You're sure nothing weird has happened?"

Where should I start? "I'm sure."

Dad sighed. "Maybe Ronald just needed a reality check."

Maybe Ronald wasn't the only one.

CHAPTER NINE

More Trouble

"Crazy night," Bailey said as she opened her front door. "I knew Ronald was mad at you, but I never thought he'd do something so stupid to get back at you. He must really belong in the psych ward."

"He's on meds," I said, determined to dodge all questions. I didn't want to stumble across a discussion about Chase, and no way could I tell her about my face-off with Ronald in the hall. Crossing the living room, I went straight for the couch.

Pade chose the spot next to me, handing me a drink as he sat down. Since Bailey sat to my other side, I quickly felt the walls closing in. The TV showed commercials on every channel as Pade hit the buttons, eventually turning off the TV and tossing the remote on the table before us.

"Bailey told me what you said at lunch."

My thoughts had been so focused on Ronald, I'd forgotten about Tosh. I shivered at the precision in his voice.

"I was upset." Pade grasped my chin, turning my face so my eyes had no place to land but on his. "I'm only going to say this one time, so I want to make sure you understand."

I tried to nod, but he didn't release my chin.

"I've never been with anyone."

"But Tosh…" I said.

He laughed bitterly and released my chin. Leaning forward, Pade dropped his head into his hands. After shaking his head and muttering under his breath, he turned to me. "Okay, let me take that back. I'll say it once more. I've. Never. Been. With. Anyone. That includes Tosh, so there's no way she's having my baby."

I sighed, filled by the pain in his words, but also a new hope radiating from my heart. Pade and I still had a chance. "Why are you telling me this?"

"So maybe you'll understand why people seem to think she is." He looked down at his hands and took a deep breath, exhaling slowly. "It's all so stupid. Not the part about what happened to Tosh, but the rumors. Let's start with July. When you were in the hospital, Tosh called and said she needed a ride. I knew it was bad—that's why I came. I just didn't realize she was being abused."

The word caught in my throat. "Abused?"

"No one knows for sure if she was actually abused," Bailey said. "Her story has already changed at least three times."

"Who abused her?" I asked.

"Her step-dad." Bailey said.

I looked at Pade. "Why would she call you?"

Pade shrugged. "I guess she didn't have anyone else to call. I drove to Credence and picked up Tosh and her mom at a gas station across town. I dropped them off with Tosh's grandmother and then went straight back to the hospital. They've been staying in a trailer on the road next to Angel's since August. No one else knows."

Bailey snickered. "No one knew until three days ago."

Pade rolled his eyes. "On Wednesday, I walked Tosh to class after lunch. She told me her mom was asking too many questions about what she told the police. Her mom might even move them back to *his* house. That's when I asked her if it really happened."

"And?" I asked, not sure if I wanted to hear the answer.

"That's when she told me she's pregnant."

"It gets worse," Bailey added.

"You know nothing stays a secret for long at Credence High." Pade cleared his throat. "Terrance overheard us talking. He heard Tosh say she was pregnant. Then he said some stuff about Tosh I won't repeat, except for the part when he said no one would claim her baby. If she even knew who it belonged to."

"And you should've kept your mouth shut, Pade Sanders," Bailey said.

"I know," he grumbled. "But Terrance has it out for me. You know he wouldn't let it go. When he looked at me and asked, 'Would you?', I couldn't think of anything else to say but 'yes'."

"Which was stupid," Bailey said. "By the end of fourth block, everyone was talking."

"Someone told Aunt Rainey," he said. "Before we got home, she'd already called Mom, and Mom had already called Dad about the 'baby'."

"Why didn't you tell your mom the truth?" I asked.

"Because it pissed me off that she didn't bother asking me before calling Dad. So, I didn't bother correcting her."

"Another stupid move." Bailey rose and disappeared into the kitchen.

"I'm sorry," he said.

I shook my head. "This is a mess."

"Dad freaked out and took the first flight in. Mom had to work this morning. She insisted we pick him up at the airport."

I took a sip of the ice-filled drink in my hand, which had numbed my fingers. "You guys are both going?"

"Pade has to drive," Bailey said, returning with a bag of chips. "You know I can't drive a stick. I also can't leave him alone with Dad. They might kill each other."

"Can I go?"

Pade looked at me. "The airport is an hour away. I don't think your parents would like that idea."

Not if they didn't know. "Mom took the boys shopping—she'll probably be gone most of the day. Dad's asleep."

"Still?" Bailey asked.

I took a long sip and chewed a piece of ice before answering. "I think he's sick again."

Pade stared at me. "Has the cancer come back?"

"I'm not sure, but I'm scared."

"I'm sorry," he said, wrapping an arm around me. "He's a fighter, Jes. Uncle Justin proved that last time."

"Is there anything I can do?" Bailey asked.

"Other than get me away from here? I don't want to be alone."

Bailey rubbed my arm. "You don't want to be near

our dad either."

"I'll take my chances."

Pade grabbed the keys from the table. "Then let's ride."

* * * * *

I scribbled a note for Dad and pinned it to the cork-board on the fridge. Hopefully we'd be back before he or Mom ever saw it.

We rode in silence, until the green signs came into view, guiding us onto the interstate.

"Last chance," Pade said.

"Are you going to tell him the truth?" I asked.

"He wouldn't believe me. This isn't about Tosh."

Dark clouds loomed above us. I felt glad Pade had installed the top. He stared ahead for miles, but he finally took his hand off the shifter and laid it on mine.

"Last year, I treated you bad. Worse than bad, I treated you like a pile of crap on the bottom of my shoe. It was all about me, and worst of all, I never stopped to think how you really felt. I just assumed you'd fall for me, like any other girl. Now I see you're the only one who was honest."

I opened my mouth, but he squeezed my hand.

"I'm so ashamed. I finally realized I treated you like my father has treated my mother all of these years. He comes and goes but doesn't seem to care that she cries when he's gone."

"We heard her, one night," Bailey said, "outside her bedroom door."

Pade nodded. "I was popular and girls wanted to date me, but none of them mattered, and then you came to Credence. You hated me at first, I could tell. I made up my mind to win you over.

"But in the end, you turned me down. I'd never felt like the world had ended. Suddenly it didn't matter what my dad said or did—all that mattered was I couldn't have you. When he told me you were sick, I packed my bags. No way could I stay there and let something bad…" He balled his fist. "I agreed to his demands. I promised not to play football anymore."

My voice felt like it belonged to someone else. "But you love football."

"When Dad asked, I didn't hesitate. He thought I just wanted to go back to Credence, to Mom. He didn't know it was all for you."

"Why?" I asked.

He stilled. "You're beautiful."

I tugged at the brown mess around my shoulders. "I'm ordinary."

"No," he said, sneaking a glance at my eyes, as if willing me to believe. "You don't understand. I'm not saying you're pretty—"

"Thanks a lot," I said.

He shook his head and placed a finger on my lips. "You're smart. You care about everything. You make my heart race when you touch my arm. Beautiful doesn't begin to describe who you really are."

I swallowed, stunned by his words. "I don't know who I am. I'm scared of my past, of not knowing what will happen if anyone finds out."

"Don't be scared," Bailey said. "You've got Pade and you've also got me. We'll take care of you, no matter what."

"But I sent you away," I said.

He grasped my hand again, bringing it to his lips. "Because you cared. I know that now."

"You don't understand." I pulled away. "I didn't want to ruin you like I ruined everyone else who loved me."

Pade laughed. "I was ruined the moment we kissed, but not in the way you think. You changed everything."

I faced the window, unable to look at him. It was more than I'd ever hoped to hear him say. And he didn't just say the words to me—he said them in front of Bailey. A tear trickled down my cheek and I wiped it away. "What will everyone at school say?"

"I only care what you say. Did you know someone has been putting hate mail in my locker? People make snarky comments in the hall. No one looks at me—all that matters is I won't play football and Credence doesn't have a chance at making state finals. So much for having friends. Where are they now?"

The jeep was silent until we pulled into the terminal.

"There he is," Bailey said.

Pade maneuvered the jeep next to the sidewalk, stopping in front of a man wearing a gray suit and a wide-brimmed hat. He turned off the jeep and climbed out, reaching for one of the man's bags.

I squinted in the sunlight, which had cut through the clouds only moments before we reached the terminal. Was he the same man I'd seen in Pade's yard the night he left Credence? I rolled down the window to get a better look.

The man approached, in no hurry. He removed his sunglasses, inspected me for a full minute, and then laughed. "So, this is the girl you knocked up?"

"Dad, I..." Pade stuttered.

"Son, you have no idea what lies ahead. If you had even an inkling about the real world, you would not be standing in front of me with this girl."

"Dad—"

"Pade, what were you thinking? Having a child now is not an option." Mr. Sanders turned to me. "How much do you want?"

"What?" I couldn't believe his words.

"How much money will it take for you to leave my son alone?"

"Dad!" Pade said. "You've got it all wrong."

The man in front of us laughed again. He turned to Pade. "I know you hate me, but you will respect me. You have so much to learn about the opposite sex. I will make your problems go away, but only this time."

"Dad," Bailey said, moaning from the backseat. "Pade has problems, but Jes isn't one of them."

The shift in Mr. Sanders' face was truly a spectacle. He looked me over again, this time taking in crucial details. When he next spoke, his voice was low and without an ounce of arrogance. "Jessica Delaney?"

"Yes," I said, despite the lump in my throat.

He tugged on his collar and turned to Pade. "Does Justin or Lorraine know she's here?"

"Not exactly," Pade said. "Jes left a note, but Uncle Justin was asleep when we left. Aunt Rainey took the boys shopping, but we'll probably be back before they are."

"We should go," Mr. Sanders said and scurried around the jeep. He lifted one of his bags into the back.

Pade carried the other bag, mumbling as he circled the jeep. I climbed into the backseat next to Bailey.

"You don't have to." Mr. Sanders motioned for me

to remain in the front seat, but I didn't move. He opened the door and pulled himself into the passenger seat. "My dear, I am truly sorry for the way I treated you." He turned around to face me. "I'm even sorrier you had to see our exchange."

I stared at the man who'd transformed from overbearing parent to somber and repentant inside of ten minutes. Someone needed to tell him the truth about Tosh, but I didn't know how to start. "Pade is a good person."

Mr. Sanders nodded. "I'm happy you still think so. His mother and I have very nearly reached our limit."

Pade didn't look at his dad as he climbed into the driver's seat.

Mr. Sanders' phone rang and he held the latest and greatest cell money could buy up to his ear. The paper-thin phone probably wasn't even on display in a store yet. "Yes, they're with me. Jessica too. We're just leaving the airport, so probably an hour." He ended the call and stared out the window.

I knew one thing without a doubt. If either Mom or Dad were on the other end of that call, I was definitely in trouble.

* * * * *

"You can't leave here without telling us," Dad roared as he paced next to the bar. "You're not eighteen yet. Hell, you're not even seventeen yet. You still have to listen to what we say."

I looked at Mom, who sat across the table. "I do listen."

"Listen and obey," he corrected. Creases formed to

the sides of his face, tightening at the corners of his eyes. "What were you thinking leaving with Pade like that?"

"Pade *and* Bailey," I corrected.

Dad frowned. "That doesn't make sneaking off any better. I find it hard to believe you'd go anywhere with Pade for two hours."

I stared at the dark circles under his eyes. "Weren't you sleeping earlier?"

"Don't change the subject," he said, struggling to pull himself away from where he'd stopped to lean against the bar.

"You *are* sick again," I said.

"That isn't your concern. Right now, we're talking about the trouble you're in."

I could not care less about the trouble. "What did the tests say?" I asked, fighting to keep the desperation out of my voice. "All your blood work must be back by now."

"Damn it." Dad shoved the red mixer from the counter. The metal bowl split off the base and rolled across the floor. The base crashed, sending ragged chunks of plastic in every direction.

Mom raised a hand to her mouth.

My eyes nearly bugged out of my head.

Dad ran a hand through his hair. When he turned back to face me, tears had filled his eyes. He knelt on the floor next to my chair, covering his face with his hands. "You act like you're worried about me and yet you run off without telling me where you are. How do you think I feel?"

I reached out to touch his shoulder.

He pulled back from my hand. "When I woke up you were gone. I tore this house apart looking for you. I didn't see the note until a half-hour later."

"I'm sorry," I said.

"Yes, I'm sick again. I told you time was running out."

I'd never hated being right this much. A horrible feeling washed over me, like a waterfall of quicksand that fell around my feet and rose up my legs, ensuring I would never escape. "I don't understand what you're saying." And I didn't care. Dad was sick again.

His eyes met mine, betraying a weakness I never wanted to see again. "All those years ago, I promised myself I'd see you through getting your memory back."

"So what if my memory never returns?" I asked.

"But it has," Mom said, "admit it."

"The dreams are getting worse," I said. "But they're just dreams."

"They torture you," Dad said. "Lorraine says you've been calling out in the night. You haven't done that since New York."

Stunned, I looked at Mom. "Why haven't you told me?"

She sighed. "I can only ask about your memory in so many ways. You've shut us out and not just since the hospital. This has gone on since last fall."

When Chase returned. "What do I call out?"

"You scream for your father—your real father. You cry out Chase's name, but we're not sure why. Maybe you should enlighten us."

I took Dad's hand in mine. "If we need to go back to Atlanta, that's fine. Chemo, radiation, whatever you need, but you've got to get treated *now*."

"It won't be that easy this time," Mom said.

Easy? She thought the chemo and radiation were

easy? What could be worse? "Mom can teach us in Atlanta. We'll stay there as long as it takes."

Dad placed his hand on my cheek. "You're willing to give up everything we've built here? We've never stayed anywhere long enough to consider it home."

"I'd give up anything for you and Mom." He had no idea I already had. I'd given up Chase and my chance at learning the truth about my past. Staring down at Dad's tired face, I felt no regrets. "I'll go upstairs and pack."

"Not yet." Dad stood. "It will take a few days to set up the treatments. We won't leave until Dr. Baynor gives the word."

I nodded, realizing I'd be the one to say goodbye to Pade and Bailey this time.

There was no other choice.

* * * * *

Danny and Collin refused to eat dinner that night.

"This is our home," Collin said, shoving his plate across the table.

Danny stood, following him to the porch. He gave me an evil look as he passed. "What did you do this time?"

I looked at Dad as the door slammed. "You're not going to tell them?"

Dad leaned back in his chair. "Not yet."

"We don't want them to worry," Mom said.

"So it's better if they hate me?"

"What do you suggest?" Dad asked.

"Honesty," I said.

Mom and Dad stared at me.

"Okay, I forgot for a second we don't do honesty in this family." I stood, shoving the chair until it slammed against the wall. "I'll check on them."

"I'll forgive you for that one," Dad mumbled.

The porch creaked under my feet as I spotted the boys at the picnic table. Without a word, I sat down next to Danny.

He pushed in his earbuds.

"You always mess up our normal," Collin said. "What happened?"

"Technically, we're not moving. We're going back to Atlanta for a while so... Dad can have more tests."

Danny pulled out one of the earbuds. "More tests?" The anger had drained from his voice. "Why does Dad need more tests?"

"We'll handle this," Dad said as he sat next to Collin.

I scooted over so Mom could sit between me and Danny.

"Your father's cancer has returned," Mom said, taking Danny's hand. "We're going back to Atlanta for more treatment."

"But... but you look fine," Danny said, staring at Dad.

"This can't be happening," Collin said, with tears in his voice.

"Some things just happen," Mom said. "We all knew the cancer could return one day. We hoped for more time, but we've had a wonderful year in Credence. Everyone at this table should be thankful for that, if nothing else."

Danny pulled out the second earbud. "How bad is it?"

Dad reached for Danny. "We've fought worse before."

"Are we moving for good?" Collin asked.

"No," Mom said, "this our home." She looked at Dad. "We'll return when your father has won the battle."

"Can we stay with Aunt Charlie during the week?" Collin asked. "At least we could stay in school. Atlanta is only two hours away."

"Maybe that would be best," Dad said.

Mom shook her head. "We will not be divided, not now." Her words seemed final as she stormed back into the house.

Dad sighed. "I'll talk to her."

CHAPTER TEN

Choices

I didn't get to see Bailey or Pade until Monday morning. Aunt Charlie and their dad insisted on 'alone time' with them, leaving Saturday afternoon before Dad finished our talk. Not a light in their house burned until ten o'clock Sunday night. I watched through the blinds as they pulled into the driveway and piled out of Aunt Charlie's car, Pade and Bailey dragging into the house behind their parents.

The week passed in our normal pattern, but neither Pade nor Bailey seemed willing to talk about their dad. I didn't bring up the fact my dad was sick again. How could I?

On Friday I sat, long after the first bell, alone against a brick wall and hunched over my knees. I failed to hear Bailey walk up.

"Hey," she said, "what's wrong?"

Looking up, I took in her completely black outfit, including the lipstick she hadn't worn in weeks. Based on her half-serious, half-teasing tone, I figured she didn't know about Dad yet.

She twisted the straps of her backpack, wrapping the ends around her fingers. "You'll never believe what my dad wants now."

I'd never seen Bailey so unsure. "For you to go back to Colorado?"

"Not yet but thank goodness he flew back last night. Pade still hasn't told him the truth." She eyed me carefully and reached for my arm. "You can't sit on that sidewalk. It's been raining all morning. Your butt will get soaked."

"Too late."

Bailey helped me to my feet. "What's wrong?"

I took a breath. Actually, I took five breaths before I could say the words without bawling. "Dad *is* sick again. Now I know for sure."

"The cancer?" she asked softly.

"Yeah."

She put an arm through mine. "I'll walk you to first block."

"No," I said, pulling back. "I've got way too much on my mind. I need time to think."

"Wait," she yelled as I ran ahead. "I need to show you something."

As I stopped, she handed me a folded piece of paper. The paper in my hand felt rough, like... newspaper. My anger exploded as I got a look at the girl at the center of the page. "Why do you have this?"

Bailey pointed to the girl's face. "There's a birthmark to the right of her eye. You can barely make it out in the picture, so I looked at it under a magnifying glass."

I squinted at the tiny brown spec. "So?"

"You don't have this birthmark. This girl isn't you."

I wanted to laugh at Bailey, arguing a point I already knew to be true. Why hadn't the New York City detectives figured it out all those years ago? "I'm not sure what you're talking about."

Bailey took the page from my hand and held it near my face. "You really don't see it?"

"Put that away," I hissed, pushing the page from my face.

Her eyes flashed bewilderment, before she refolded the page. "Here," she said, as if the newspaper was no more than a wrapper from a stick of gum she would toss in the nearest trashcan.

Guilt flowed through me as I grabbed the page, but only for a few seconds. Why had she dug into my past? The box was my mystery to solve, not hers. "Thanks," I said, shooting her a look of disgust. "I don't need your help getting to class."

"Fine then," she said and left me standing near the entrance to building three.

Again, a needle of guilt tingled inside, for her words vented hurt instead of anger. I slipped the page into my purse.

Inside the doors, at the entrance to the girls' bathroom, Brianna Lars stood with her hands on her hips. Rachelle cowered in front of her. Both looked up as I walked by.

"So," Brianna said, "it's the freak."

I froze. Why had she called me that?

Brianna grinned. "Then you admit it? Freak."

Rachelle lowered her eyes to the floor and crept backward a few inches.

"Why are you messing with me?" I asked.

"Because I now know how you messed with me." She gripped her collar, pulling it tight against her neck.

My stomach turned over and over as I fought the fear that gripped me, holding my body like a statue.

Her smile grew. "You can't hide the truth from me."

"Can I go now?" Rachelle asked, without looking up.

"For now," Brianna said, her laugh almost a cackle.

"What's going on?" I asked Rachelle.

A lump formed in my throat as she grabbed her bag and ran down the hall. I looked to my left and right. Either way, the hall was empty. Every door had closed after the late bell.

"I'll tell you what's going on," Brianna said, gripping my wrist.

I struggled under her grip, but Brianna's fingers tightened. Her face was focused, revealing not a hint of strain.

"I can bench press half your weight or more, in case you're wondering."

Again, I looked nervously down the empty hall. How could I get away from her? Maybe my power…

Brianna shoved the door behind her and pulled me into the bathroom. As soon as the door closed, she released my hand. "Go ahead. Show me what Jes Delaney can do."

I rubbed the red marks on my wrist. "I don't know what you're talking about."

"Come on, Jes." She pushed me with both hands.

My back slammed against the wall, along with my head, making a 'thud' sound that echoed through my head. My purse and backpack dropped to the floor. A pain shot from behind my ears, like a laser beam straight to my eyes.

"Make something happen. I dare you."

I considered her dare. No one would know. We were alone. Or were we? Out of the corner of my eye, I noticed something move. Craning my neck to look around Brianna, I saw the edge of a red shirt, peaking out of the last stall. And in the outstretched hand... a phone.

Gathering all of my strength, I turned one foot sideways, bracing against the wall, and shoved my shoulder into Brianna's chest.

She doubled over in a fit of coughs, straining to catch her breath. Ronald rushed out of the stall, still holding his phone. He stopped about a foot from me and looked from my face to Brianna's. Seeing my window of opportunity disappear, I ran out of the bathroom.

I didn't stop until I reached history class. As I grasped the door handle, I realized my purse and backpack were still in the bathroom. I looked back down the hall, but no one had emerged from the bathroom door.

I opened the door to history class and took my usual seat in the back.

* * * * *

Pushing open the bathroom door, I tiptoed in, not sure what, or who awaited me. Near one of the sinks sat my purse, with all of the contents dumped into a messy pile nearby. The books from my backpack had been removed and the pages torn out. The notebooks, retaining only their metal rings, laid open on the floor near the square drain at the bathroom's center. Dozens of pages of notebook paper with my handwriting spread across the floor, into the stalls, and even filled the toilets.

I shook my head at the mess, not knowing where to start. Opening my wallet, I was shocked to see the twenty. But then, they weren't after money. Brianna and Ronald—that was a twisted combination. But Rachelle? What had I done to deserve Rachelle playing their game?

Scraping the makeup and notes from the floor and back into my purse, I sighed. The bathroom door opened and sounds of laughter floated in, along with two voices. Thankfully, neither belonged to Brianna or Ronald. I scrambled to get all of the dry pages back into my notebooks. The wet pages from the floor found a new home in the trash. The ones in the toilet… well, even the cleaning obsession Mom had branded into me over the years had limits.

Lunch consisted of Angel talking about Skip. They were on. No, they were off. I'm not sure even Angel knew what they were. The pizza on my plate turned cold as I stared at Rachelle. She ate every last bite of her pizza as she nodded along with Angel's story, even laughed a few times.

Rachelle never met my eyes.

After school, I walked to the locker, all the way preparing myself for how to confront Rachelle. Two girls passed me in the hall, pointing and giggling as I walked by.

A guy passed with a roll of his eyes and a snicker. The hall was empty up ahead. I released a breath, for I wouldn't have to face Rachelle yet.

The relief was short-lived as I noticed the outline of

a piece of paper, taped to my locker door. With every step, an apprehension grew inside that took me back over twelve years of fear. Taped to the door of my locker was a picture of Jessica Naples, hugging her teddy bear. I ripped the picture loose and held the crisp white paper in my hands.

Someone had the picture, and they'd made a copy.

Under the picture, Naples was marked out. Delaney was written after Jessica in large letters. I squinted, trying to make out the writing at the top of the page.

Lost girl—want one?

What was it with bullies and making my life suck? Not only was Brianna making fun of me, she'd found a way to torture me about something that never happened. I crunched the paper into a ball, squeezing with all of my strength. If only I had the strength to deliver a blow to Brianna Lars in the bathroom, she would not have this picture.

Tears burned in my eyes, tears of anger. This was Bailey's fault. No, this was my fault. I never should have told her the truth. The tears welled, threatening to fall. How could Rachelle stab me in the back when the only thing clear to me was the fact she hated Brianna?

Unsure of what to do next, I ran down the hall toward the office. Mom always stopped to see Dr. Greene after school, even when there was no meeting. She would know what to do. My feet came to a halt as reality hit. She would want to move again. It was always her solution before, whenever someone started asking questions my parents didn't want to answer.

But I didn't have a choice. Too many people had already seen the picture. The girl's name was Jessica, and that was enough. It wasn't me, but would Brianna care if

I told her the truth? No, she'd laugh in my face. Squaring my shoulders, I walked toward the office.

Another copy of the picture hung on the cafeteria door. I pulled it down, crushing it also. To my left, the computer lab overflowed with laughter. I forced myself through the crowd at the door but choked as I stared at the computer screens. An entire row of monitors stretched along the wall, each with a duplicate screen. Jessica Naples cried on every one.

Escaping into the hall, I ran for the main doors. Everyone who passed stared. The tears were now flowing freely down my cheeks. Around the last corner, I skidded to a stop in front of Mom and Dr. Greene.

"What is going on?" Mom asked, holding up the picture.

Dr. Greene's eyes darted from me to the picture. "Lorraine, is there something you'd like to tell me?"

"Not really," she said. "But if you must know—yes, it's her. I don't know how this article came to reside within the walls of Credence High." Mom glared at me. "Or why the students must make such a fuss."

Dr. Greene rubbed his chin. "I seem to recall this story." He looked at the paper. "About twelve years ago? Yes, I remember all the coverage. The girl disappeared for a week. First the parents did it. Then they found the girl running down a highway barefoot—guy almost ran her over with a truck. I wouldn't remember if it wasn't so damned strange."

"The guy in the truck was Justin."

His eyes opened wider than I thought possible. "You're kidding me."

I blinked. Did Mom just admit the truth? After all those years of lying?

She looked at me again. "Tell me how this got here."

"Bailey found the article in the shed she brought it and…" I took a breath, "it was in my purse and… Brianna and Ronald cornered me in the bathroom and dumped out my bag and…" I took another breath, "now everyone in school knows. They must have made a thousand copies."

"Jes," Mom said, "you never do anything halfway."

The room spun around me. Laughter sounded from all directions. I sat on the stairs behind Mom. Why was all of this happening?

"Calm down." Dr. Greene looked at Mom. "What is she talking about?"

Mom held the article in one hand and pointed at the picture with the other. "This is Jes at four," she said, as if telling him again might make him believe.

But it really wasn't me. Why didn't she tell him the truth?

"I never knew you lived in New York."

"For a while." She sighed. "Joel, we've kept this secret for a long time to protect Jes. Her real parents disappeared shortly before Justin and I adopted her. The last thing we needed was the media butting in."

"Yes," he said gravely. "Cameras are the last thing we need around here."

"I'm sorry," she said.

Dr. Greene looked at his watch. "Go home. It's Friday. Surely by Monday morning this will have made way for more delicious drama."

"It won't go away," I whispered.

Mom grabbed my arm and pulled me up to stand. "He's right. We'll give it some time."

There would never be enough time.

* * * * *

Dad was asleep when we got home, which meant something good had finally happened that day. Everything before I stepped out of the van that evening would remain unsaid, until a time when Dad insisted on hearing the story. Never telling him suited me just fine.

I thought about the article, marked with words that had infuriated me. Brianna was smart—after the bathroom, she probably raced for the nearest computer. Within an hour, she knew all about my past.

No way could I go back to that on Monday morning. If only we were ready to pack for Atlanta. But Mom had said it would probably be Wednesday at the earliest.

Lying across my bed, I wanted to cry, though I'd cried on the way home until the skin around my eyes felt like a sponge.

My life finally, without a doubt, one hundred percent totally sucked.

A single tear slipped down my cheek, but it wasn't because of the day, or because of Bailey's stupidity, or even Rachelle's willingness to stab me in the back. It wasn't because Dad was sick.

The tear was for Chase, who had turned his back on me. He promised one day I'd agree to return to his planet because I wanted to. Maybe that day had arrived. I cradled the charm in my hand. Maybe I had the power to leave this mess and never look back. After everyone went to bed, I'd press the green stone.

Dinner that night was one of the worst Mom had

ever made. She burned the green beans, after dumping them from a can. The heap of salt in the mashed potatoes tingled the insides of my mouth. The chicken was dry and I reached for a greasy dark piece, only to be beat out by the boys. Even so, I ate every bite, slowly savoring this last meal with my family.

I hugged Mom and Dad extra tight before I climbed the stairs. I said I loved them.

In the doorway to the boys' room, I watched as the twins played a video game. Focused on the TV, they never noticed I stood only feet away.

Back in my room, I filled my purse with small reminders of them all. If only Mom believed in taking pictures. Then I realized I never got the chance to ask about her sister. My heart filled with regret over this small conversation, knowing I'd lost my chance.

No, I couldn't regret going home. I had to find Chase.

I reached for the glasses Chase gave me and the book I'd kept for almost a year. Moving aside the clothes in my top dresser drawer, I lifted the copy of *Pride and Prejudice* Mrs. Pearson had left with me. I opened to a spot in the middle of the book and read one of the handwritten notes. The words were in *her* language. The smell of old paper made me warm inside.

She'd love to have the book back, I was sure. Maybe returning it was my duty. In that moment, holding the book that probably belonged to my mother, I realized I no longer needed it. Before the night's end, I would hopefully see her again. If I returned the book, she would be happy. She'd said it was one of her favorites. But if I didn't return it—well, that might give me a reason to come back one day. I put the book in the drawer and covered it with my clothes.

My phone buzzed on the dresser. Bailey had sent a text. There was a party Saturday night at Terrance's house. She and Pade were invited. They wanted me to come. After the whole school found out about Jessica Naples? No way.

I considered a response for ten minutes but pressed the 'off' button instead. Maybe I should take the phone. What would it hurt? I laughed at myself when I realized it wouldn't work in space. Who needed a cell phone when Chase had fancy gadgets that made our phones seem more like those flip phones on TV from the nineteen eighties?

When the floor below fell into a silent darkness, I stood before my window. The sky was clear above, filled with stars that glittered along the horizon, but no moon. I stared at the house next door, thinking of Bailey and then of Pade. Their windows were dark and murky, showing no sign of life. Was Bailey still mad at me? Would they ever forgive me for leaving?

Could I get over loving Pade from a million miles away?

Crossing to my closet, I drew out my warmest sweater, for the September nights had turned cold, as if already welcoming fall. Slipping the knitted fusion of blue and green over my head, I reached for a scarf and hat Mom had insisted on buying during our last shopping trip. It would be cold in the woods, not freezing, but chilly enough to make goosebumps rise along my arms.

I had no idea how long I'd need to stand by the creek.

With a deep breath, I closed my eyes. Imagining the

sound of rushing water, I opened my eyes to the creek, not ten feet before me. I scanned the bushes along the creek for movement, any hint that a life other than me might be breathing the crisp night air.

"Hello," I said, but only the water answered.

I shivered, wondering what I would do if the coyote returned, or worse. My power almost failed me the last time.

"Chase," I said as a gentle breeze blew my hair against my face. Pulling the hat down over my ears, I scanned the tops of the trees. Branches reached like hands for the stars, which twinkled with an intensity that only grew as the air began to cool. Even without the moon, the ground around my feet glowed in the white light. With all the man-made lights in our Atlanta neighborhood, I never got to see the stars wrap around the earth. An endless night, stretching without threat of city lights in all directions.

My toes ached to step into the water one last time. Good thing my head registered the fact it was way too cold.

I spun, taking in three hundred and sixty degrees of beauty I'd never see again. Pulling the charm from under my sweater, I pressed the green center.

"Chase," I said again, but the breeze had become a strong current of air that carried my words away. My heart picked up speed as I wondered if Chase would come. I never allowed myself to consider any other possibility before.

"That didn't take long," said a voice from behind me.

Turning, I flung my arms around Chase.

CHAPTER ELEVEN

Return To The Past

"You remembered?" Chase asked, as he stepped back and looked over me. "Everything?"

"Only that night." I placed a hand on his cheek. My fingers couldn't lie. Chase was really there.

"Why did you leave me?" he asked, holding his breath.

"I never meant to leave. I followed our father, sure he'd return once he found me on the ship. But then you were taken…"

Chase released the breath and closed his eyes, as if experiencing that night all over again.

"Was that your mother?" I asked.

His eyes flew open. "It was her sister. You really don't remember? She hates Mom, but we can talk about that later."

"What did she—?"

"Mom got me back, and nothing else matters."

Sorrow washed over me as my thoughts took me back to that night. "Our father, he…"

"I know," Chase said. He gripped my shoulders. "Don't say the words. I've waited a long time for this."

"Will you take me back?"

He smiled. "I thought you'd never ask." Reaching forward, he took my hand and closed his eyes. When he opened them, we stood inside of a room not much larger than the van.

My head bumped against an overhead compartment outlining a door with a square handle.

"Be careful," Chase said as he ducked and moved toward the front, slightly hunched over. He slid into one of two seats. Motioning to the other, I sat beside him, in a seat that felt softer than one of the feather pillows I loved to sleep with.

"You've got questions," he said.

Taking a full look around, I nodded, unsure of where to begin. Black glass filled the space to our front and sides, even the ceiling and narrow sections of the floor. It was the same black glass I remembered from the ship the night I left Golvern, and the night a year ago when Chase almost took me back.

Reaching for the controls, Chase pressed several buttons and a soft humming noise sounded to either side of us. The panel in front of us pulsed to life, flashing a mixture of pink and green lights. The glass before us began to glow.

"How does this work? What kind of power does it use?" I asked.

He punched a flashing green button and the humming noise stopped. "Let's get off the ground first."

I looked at the simple armrests to either side of the seat. "Should I grab onto something? Maybe put on a seat belt?"

"This ride will be nothing like the movies."

Gripping the armrests, I closed my eyes, not wanting to hyperventilate, but the space was too confined. I had no idea what to expect next. Seconds passed and nothing happened.

"You can let go," Chase said.

"I've only been on a plane twice, but I remember takeoff was the worst."

"Jes," he said, "calm down. We're already in the air."

Opening my eyes, my breathing stopped. Surrounding us, the black glass had 'turned on' like a TV screen. To either side of us, the night sky stretched to the horizon of starts. Below our feet, the tops of trees waved as we sped by.

"You're turning blue," Chase said.

Coughing, I reached forward and touched the screen. My fingers pressed against the smooth glass. "It's not even warm."

"Power-saving technology. You could run these screens off less power than it takes to charge your cell phone."

I reached for my purse, forgetting for a moment I had left my phone. There was no way to call home and no chance of turning back. We rose higher, the trees below fading to dots and then darkness. Up ahead, the edge of the sky glowed with a light that brightened as we approached.

"Atlanta," he said.

Even though it felt as if we sat still, tiny dots of light along the highway below us seemed to crawl. I jerked, letting out a tiny yelp as I noticed a plane to my right. Some of the windows were lit—I squinted, trying to make out people on the other side. "Can they see us?"

Chase maneuvered us closer to the plane, laughing as I squirmed. "We're hidden from human technology."

I thought about all the planes I remembered in the sky over Atlanta. "What if we get in their way?"

"I'm actually a decent pilot, although you can't tell the difference yet."

"I can't believe you can fly a spaceship," I said, shaking my head. "My parents won't even let me get a driver's license."

"You'll have to work on mentioning your parents. Mom won't be happy hearing you refer to them."

"But they did raise me." And I already missed my family.

Chase didn't say anything, only stared ahead.

I needed to change the subject. "Were you really in history class or did I imagine that?"

"I was there."

"But no one saw you."

He turned around in his seat to face me. "You did."

"But how?"

"Let's try a subject that's… a little safer. Let's start with why I didn't return last year."

Oh yeah, that was really safe. "Okay, why didn't you return?"

"All of the tests said you weren't Kayden. To be more specific, the tests didn't one-hundred percent rule you out, but it wasn't what Mom had hoped for. You should have been the exception to the rule. She decided to keep looking."

My stomach felt like I never wanted to eat again. "She never believed like you did."

"I was sure and I wanted to come back, but I

couldn't convince her to let me go. Mom asked that I never bring up your name again."

"Because she hated me."

"Because she was heartbroken. She never admitted it, but I believe she wanted you to be Kayden too. I finally convinced her to let me come back. She restarted the search in New York since that's where our father's ship crashed. It's how he died."

"Crashed?" I'd dreamed of that night, remembering hundreds of small pieces, images that seemed to finally link together in the hospital. Then the day Collin was hurt—there was a gun, screaming, and more than enough blood. But nowhere in the deepest pits of my memory was a crash.

"I came back to Credence to check on you right before school started. That's when I overheard someone mention your coma."

"I was in the hospital for two months."

"But from a sunburn? No normal human would be comatose over a sunburn. For the first time in months, the world around me felt right."

Something about his words bothered me. "You said your mom was in New York—"

"Our mom," he corrected.

I stared at Chase. "But you said I wasn't—"

"According to the tests last year, you weren't. Turns out there was a problem with the algorithm. Our doctor believed a bone sample would tell us the truth about you, without making you return to Golvern. You played the guilt card like a pro with Mom, but the answer was there the whole time." He smiled. "I told you before— computers are stupid. Our computers are more advanced than Earth computers, but some of our people believe they can make electronics interpolate real decision making. One wrong entry by a junior staff member, one wrong decision made, and the errors become exponential."

"So, I *am* Kayden?"

He looked at me strangely. "You tell me."

I closed my eyes and gripped the necklace. "Yes."

"You said that with real confidence. I'm proud of you. Too bad no one else knew the truth until a few days ago. We got the message right after Renora's assignment ended."

"Who?"

"Your history teacher."

I stared at him.

Chase laughed. "You thought she was Mom, didn't you? Well, she does work for Mom and she is mean, like I said. Her mission was to check on you." Chase smiled. "Mom was underhanded about the whole thing. She insisted you weren't on her mind, but then she sent her first lieutenant to make sure you were okay. I wasn't supposed to know."

"I thought Mrs. Austen had to be Mrs. Pearson."

"Why?"

"Because of the name, Mrs. Austen."

"Mom chose the name after some author. I'm not sure why, but she insisted Renora use that name."

"When you were in Credence last fall, she gave me a copy of *Pride and Prejudice*, written by Jane Austen. She said it was her favorite book."

His eyes doubled in size. "The one with leaves on the spine?"

"Yes. She wanted me to read it for a book report."

"She's always carried that book wherever she went.

I asked about it a few months ago, when I didn't see it on her dresser. Mom said she lost it. I've thought about finding her another copy, but that one was really old. It was a gift from our father."

The sadness in his voice brought me back to what he said about history class. "Why did Mrs. Austen act like she didn't know who you were?"

"Because she didn't know I was there."

How could she not see him? "I don't understand."

"It's what you would think of as a hologram. I was never supposed to be in that room, and technically I wasn't. What you saw was a visual projection of myself."

"Why was I the only one?"

"I knew it was you, Kayden. I never doubted that fact, but I used the hologram as a way to test my theory. It was bio-metrically coded."

"Which means?"

"Only someone with my DNA could see me—can't get much closer than a twin. I designed it to test on you."

"Then you knew the truth the first day of class."

"I did, but remember—I was never actually in that room. I couldn't tell anyone, especially not Mom. If she refused to listen, I'd lose my chance. Instead, I combed the computer program until I found the mistake. I insisted they run your DNA tests again. The results came back two days ago. You're Kayden."

Something still bothered me. "How did Ronald see you?"

"You're overthinking this. I allowed Ronald to see me because I wasn't sure what he planned to do to you. At that point, I no longer needed the coding. I knew who you were."

Below us, the lights of Atlanta became sparse neighborhoods, and then random dots until mostly darkness surrounded the ship. I tapped my foot against the black glass below me, just to be sure it still separated me from the ground. "When are we going higher?"

"We won't be leaving the atmosphere tonight."

He wasn't taking me back to Golvern? "Where are we going?"

"New York." He pressed three buttons on the panel. The stars in the sky before us seemed to tilt. "We're going to where all of this started—maybe then you'll get your memory back."

I looked at Chase, staring down at the panel, his fingers flexing as if he wanted to say more. His arms bulged under his shirt.

"You looked like our teacher," I said. "In your hologram."

"Yeah, I changed a few things. Since no one else could see me, I didn't want to take a chance on you screaming my name in the middle of class."

I squeezed his arm. "But these are real."

Chase smiled "I've been working out, training for… Jes, we've got so much to talk about. We…" He turned to me. "I'm sorry, Kayden—it feels so good to say your name without a flood of tears."

"Not much chance of that," I said as tears sprang to my eyes, matching his. "Maybe next time."

* * * * *

Up ahead, the lights grew stronger, until every inch of the sky was filled by a glow from the city below. The glow surpassed what Atlanta boasted, and all other cities combined as we flew above. I didn't need to ask if this was New York City.

Chase brought the ship lower so that we cruised level with the tops of skyscrapers. He made the ship dance between the towers, circling some, and then abruptly dropped to a hover above a crowded street.

I gripped the armrests, not caring if I couldn't feel our descent. It was enough to see the yellow taxis rushing up at us.

"Scared?" Chase asked.

"A little," I said, hoping he couldn't hear my teeth chatter.

"How about I go a *little* faster?" Chase hit a button and music played, filling the ship with a jam as if a normal radio with real speakers hid behind the controls. He hit another button and the we sped forward, dodging street lamps and bridges, with glass storefronts to either side as we accelerated through the narrow streets. Down an alleyway, I closed my eyes, only to open them as we emerged in Times Square, nearly slamming into a red and white Coke ad. Just before we reached the glowing surface, the ship tilted up, and we shot straight for the sky.

"Had enough?" Chase laughed with real amusement.

"Yes," I screamed. "This is crazy. I see us moving, my head tells my stomach I should be sick, but we don't actually move."

"We *are* moving, but the stabilizers keep gravity in a perfect balance."

"Weird," I said.

"You'll get used to it," he said as the ship leveled off and brought the Statue of Liberty into our sights.

"Slow down," I begged as we approached. "I've never seen her up close."

Chase took the ship in smoothly, with three revolutions from her torch down to her sandals, ensuring I got the best close-up ever.

Eventually, he brought the ship over a dimmer edge of the city and descended to a street between two rows of houses with black roofs. As we slowed to land on the pavement, I shivered. The house in front of us... I'd seen it before.

The last time was in an article. The woman had stood before this house for an interview, begging for the return of her daughter. Cameras flashed before her face. Her husband stood to her side, with tears of support.

Chase grabbed my hand. "We'll be on the street in a minute. Don't forget to stand."

Even with his warning, I stumbled as my feet materialized on the pavement. Two men in black suits rushed forward to steady me. "What's going on?" I asked, pulling from their grasp, which brought up not-so-fond memories of being taken against my will.

Waving them back, Chase pulled me toward the house. "They work for Mom."

Looking around, I counted at least twenty people standing between us and the house, watching as we walked up the steps. The concrete felt uneven and I almost fell, but Chase's strong arms guided me to the door. A woman in a black suit opened the screen door and moved to the side as we passed.

Two more men in black suits stood to either side of the door. One whispered to the other, but I couldn't make out his words.

"What's with all the black suits?" I asked.

"Anyone driving by would probably think detectives or agents of some kind."

I looked around at the green and orange wallpaper, taking in the dolls and toy keyboard swept into a pile at one corner. Peeking into the kitchen, I saw the ragged cabinet doors, some hanging from their hinges. Dirt and toys and broken plates sat in neat piles, again swept into the corners.

"This way." The woman pointed to the living room.

Recognizing her voice, I turned to get a good look at her brown hair, twisted in a ball above her head. It was the woman who pretended to be my history teacher.

Inside the living room, I froze as my eyes landed on a woman sitting on the couch. She stared at me with a tired and somewhat sad look in her eyes. Wrinkled skin hung low around her face—she was older than the pictures, but no one could mistake her eyes.

Turning to Chase, I realized he still held my hand. "What's going on?"

He put a finger to his mouth.

"Tell the story for us again, Mrs. Naples," said a firm, clear voice that I'd also heard before.

I put a hand over my mouth as I spotted Mrs. Pearson leaning against the far wall. It occurred to me that many nights would pass before I could call her anything but Mrs. Pearson. Her arms were crossed and her full attention was on Marsha Naples.

"This pains me," Marsha said.

"Once again," Mrs. Pearson said. "Please."

"My daughter, Jessica Naples, died the night I reported her kidnapped."

"Tell us more," Mrs. Pearson said.

"It was an accident. Frank and I never meant

for…" Tears filled Marsha's eyes. Her hands shook as she gripped the Styrofoam cup in her hand. Tighter, her fingers squeezed until the cup split and the contents spilled into her lap.

I reached forward to help her, why I'm not sure. Maybe it was instinct. Maybe I felt sorry for her. Chase tightened his grip on my hand. Steam rose from the liquid soaking into the woman's pants, but she didn't move.

"I'm sorry." Marsha put her head in her hands.

"We need more," Mrs. Pearson said, striding forward to loom over her, at the same time handing her a stack of napkins from the coffee table.

"No," I said.

She looked at me. "This is important. You need to know what really happened that night."

This time Chase released my hand. I backed up, but stopped when my shoe slammed against a baseboard.

Mrs. Pearson approached, cautiously. "I want you to be sure this woman is not your mother."

I took another look at Marsha Naples. The napkins were balled up in her lap, but she didn't seem to notice or try to clean herself. She muttered about her only daughter, about how her baby was gone. Jessica was never coming back.

Pulling myself from the wall, I pushed past Mrs. Pearson and shoved open the front door. The guards moved out of my way without a word. I hadn't noticed how cold the air outside felt until after standing in that hundred-degree room. I drew a breath of the air and released the tension inside of me as I lowered to my knees on the pavement.

Steps sounded behind me.

"This is more than you can handle," Mrs. Pearson said. "We will try again tomorrow."

Tomorrow? I was never going through that again. "I don't care what happened to Jessica Naples."

"What did you say?" she whispered.

Turning, I looked up at her. "I'm not Jessica Naples, and I'd honestly rather *not* know the truth about what happened to her. I have enough nightmares already."

Mrs. Pearson dropped to her knees in front of me. "You remembered?"

I considered the raw emotion in her voice—the desperation, the hope. "I remember getting on the ship. I wasn't kidnapped…"

"Kayden…" she said.

I nodded.

Her lower lip quivered as her eyes filled with tears. She bit down on her lip. "I feared never seeing you again. You cannot understand what it feels like to lose a child."

I swallowed back the ache in my throat. "I know how it felt to lose you and Chadsworth."

"Why couldn't that part stay hidden?" Chase asked, from the porch.

Mrs. Pearson, my mother, opened her arms, though her face revealed hesitation. Anxiety. Fear.

Inching forward, I sat perfectly still as her arms touched my shoulders. For a moment, she closed her eyes and ran her hands up and down my arms. Those hands began to shake, reaching further around me, enveloping me as if I were made of glass. As her arms tightened and her shoulders relaxed, gentle sobs began.

The sound was sad, bringing me to tears, as I

inhaled the lavender smell I remembered from all those years ago. It was her.

Mrs. Pearson had been my mother all along.

Leaning forward, I buried my head in her chest, crying as she touched my hair, my face, and kissed my forehead.

The street had emptied around us. Even Chase had disappeared, leaving us to this moment, a reunion twelve years in the making.

"Mom," I whispered.

She smiled through her tears and hugged me again.

CHAPTER TWELVE

More Secrets

"He won't hurt you," Chase said.

Standing next to Chase, I made no attempt to approach the bed, which looked softer than it actually was. "You said that last time."

The doctor wore the same white suit as the night Chase tried to kidnap me. "I can do this with you standing, but you'll be more comfortable sitting on the bed."

Chase gave my arm a squeeze for support, but I pulled away and stomped over to the bed. "Fine, run your tests." Why did they insist on checking me out when I felt fine?

Tapping on a device that looked like a tablet, the doctor gave a faint smile. "This won't hurt a bit."

I rolled my eyes. "Is that universal doctor-talk?"

This time he laughed. Drawing a circle in the air, the room darkened and a light shot down from the ceiling, surrounding me and expanding to a three-foot circle around my feet. Sparkles spun across my shoes, morphing from blue to red and then green, finally fading to a solid white light.

"Look at me," I grumbled, "the Christmas tree. Want me to hold still?"

"Sure," he said.

Minutes passed as I fought the urge to move, until a cramp seized my neck. I rubbed my neck, fighting against the cramp that grew stronger as I tilted my head. "Can I move now?"

"You could move before," the doctor said.

"Why did you tell me to hold still?"

He shrugged. "Sounded good." Reaching for my arm, he scraped the surface of my skin with some type of scalpel.

"Ouch," I whined, but his eyes were trained on the knife.

The doctor placed the scraping on a white counter with a series of black circles, like the top of a stove. The sample rested at the center of one of the circles and I wondered why he didn't use a petri dish. "Amazing," he said as the circle lit up.

I turned to Chase. "How can I understand him? Does everyone on this ship speak English?"

Chase nodded. "Our language on Golvern is complex, but it's only one compared to thousands of languages on Earth. Whenever a team is assigned to an Earth mission, they spend the first twenty days learning the most popular language of their destination."

"How did you learn?" I asked.

"TV shows, movies, books. The Internet. Anything I could download I read, which is why I sound nothing like Mom. She sticks to that Shakespeare junk."

"Shakespeare is better than anything on the

Internet," said a voice from the doorway. "How is she?"

"Excellent," the doctor said, "which I find extraordinarily hard to believe with the radiation on this planet." He shivered. "It's everywhere—in the air, seeping from the food supply."

"But you have more," she said.

"Oh yes," he said, with a goofy grin. "I couldn't believe the level of health your daughter has maintained, until I found this…" Touching the screen, he stepped back as a string of blue molecules appeared.

"What is that?" Chase asked, shoving me aside to get a better look.

The doctor pointed to several locations on the screen, using a series of words I didn't understand. "Truthfully," he finally said, "I'm not sure. It was covering Kayden's skin."

"Sunscreen," I said.

Shaking his head violently, the doctor stabbed at the screen as if upset at my suggestion. "This is no human product. These chemicals are a thousand years more advanced."

"Can you determine the purpose?" my mother asked. "Can you replicate it?"

He threw his hands over his face, seeming to understand for the first time. His voice shook as he spoke. "You have no idea what your daughter has discovered. If I can replicate it, I will. We need more."

She looked at me strangely and then back at him. "Why?"

"Because this is what has kept your daughter alive all of these years."

"Sunscreen?" she asked.

"I told you," he said, with a dose of urgency.

"Humans did not make this. A team on Golvern has spent years attempting to synthesize a barrier to protect us from Earth's sun. If only such a chemical could be designed… and your daughter walks on board with it coating her skin."

"It doesn't make sense," I said.

"It healed you," Chase said, eyes wide with excitement. "Do you know what this means? We could visit Earth without having a deadline to return."

Mrs. P—my mother's expression was unreadable. "I will be in my office," she said and turned for the door.

* * * * *

Following Chase down the long hall, I recognized most of the ship that almost took me home last fall. Black glass extended along the walls and ceiling, with no reflection. The people we passed wore green uniforms that covered everything but their hands and face. Some stopped to stare, whispering as we passed the door to the control room where I once convinced Mrs. Pearson I wasn't her daughter. My mother. Mom. Instead of picturing her in my mind, I saw Lorraine.

Guilt swept over me. Lorraine would always be Mom. Somehow, I must find a way to think of Mrs. Pearson as my mother. She deserved my love, including the chance to know me and make up for the last twelve years.

A gap formed between me and Chase. I ran ahead to catch up, but I couldn't stop thinking about Mom. Had she and Dad found me missing yet? "What time is it?"

"Two o'clock in Credence," Chase said, without

looking back.

Another woman in green whispered to a man, both scattering as I acknowledged them. "Did you hear what they said?"

Chase stopped before a door with a square handle. He touched the handle and the door opened. We stepped into a room surrounded by the familiar black glass, with a desk and a black office chair that seemed almost human. Mrs. Pearson sat in the chair, drinking what looked like a cup of coffee.

She noticed me looking at the chair. "This is one of only a handful of treasured items I brought back from Earth."

Looking around the room, my eyes stopped on a white frame along the wall of glass to her right. Within the frame hung a penciled drawing of a creek. Crossing over to it, I touched the glass that protected the drawing I'd made for Chase last fall. Closing my eyes, I pictured the water, the smell of pine trees. The smooth rocks beneath my feet. "I can't believe you kept this."

"It may be hard for you to believe, but you were never far from my mind."

I thought about what Chase said in the hall. Two o'clock. Enough time for me to sneak back into my room, without anyone knowing I left. If only I could have one more day with my parents to explain why I had to leave.

Taking one of two metal seats in front of her, I inhaled the steam that rose from the cup that waited for me. The yellow liquid looked like mustard, but with the sweetness of an orange and the spicy, pungent aroma of hot wings.

"This was your favorite drink," she said.

Chase sat to my right. "You first."

Lifting the cup to my lips, I took a small sip, coughing on the explosion of taste in my mouth. Instead of one flavor, the foamy drink seeped a thousand tiny bursts against my tongue, leaving me cozy and energized at the same time.

"What does it taste like?" she asked.

"Everything," I said, downing the rest of the cup.

"Easy with that," Chase said. "It does the same thing to your insides."

Wiping my lips with my arm, I leaned back in the chair and stared at the woman before me.

She took a sip, trying not to meet my eyes. "This is strange for you, but your honesty may help our situation."

"I'm trying to figure out what to call you."

"Evelyn." She looked up at me. "First call me by my name. One day we shall figure out the rest."

I nodded. Evelyn I could do. "What is my real name? My dad said I once insisted on him calling me Kay Ray, but he thought Kay was short for Jessica."

"You are Kayden Raven Draigon."

"Seriously?" I asked, turning to Chase. "And you complained about Chadsworth. Bullies are creative with Delaney, but I can only guess what they'll make out of Draigon."

"No one will make fun of your name here," Chase said. "Everyone likes Mom."

"I meant to ask about that. Does everyone here work for you?"

"Yes," she said, but offered nothing more.

Silence settled over the room as Chase and Evelyn finished their drinks. A faint beeping sounded from one of the instrument panels, but neither moved. Finally, she pointed and the noise disappeared.

"Why did you point?" I asked. "You didn't need to."

"You might call such a thing consideration," she said.

"Considering what?"

"No," Chase said. "Consideration, like being respectful. On Golvern, most people have the same power, so we try to let someone know before we use it."

"You said most, but not everyone?"

"Other powers are rare but do exist." He smiled. "Have you found any new powers?"

"Yeah, right. I worked hard enough to figure out how to move stuff again."

"Your powers did not return because of hard work," Evelyn said. "The treatment for your sunburn reactivated them."

I crossed and then uncrossed my legs, unable to find a comfortable position. "The woman in the hall said something that sounded like 'Honra Ril.' So did someone at the house. I thought I imagined it at first, but this time I was sure. What does it mean?"

Evelyn frowned. "You were given that name, but not by one of us."

"It doesn't translate to English," Chase said.

"Try," I insisted.

Chase sighed. "In literal terms, Honra Ril means leftover girl. You might refer to Honra as a 'loose end.' Others have either been lost or disappeared during missions on Earth."

The night was getting stranger with every second. "Why would they whisper about me?"

"Most of the people on this ship know we came to Earth seeking Kayden," Evelyn said. "No doubt, the rumors have spread fast through the night."

"What does it matter if they know?" I asked, remembering the time Chase thought I might be in danger. "Does someone want me to stay hidden?"

"They're called the Lucha Noir," he offered.

"Chadsworth!" Her voice was bitter. "You will only hurt Kayden more."

Chase closed his eyes and a full cup appeared before each of us. "You suggested honesty. She deserves the truth."

For a moment, they stared at each other, waiting for someone to flinch.

"Enough." I jumped to my feet. "Someone please tell me what's going on." I looked at Evelyn. "Start by telling me who you really are. Then tell me why it matters who I am."

"You matter because of me. You already noticed I am the leader here."

Chase shoved his chair back. "And you worried *I* might hurt her."

"Sit back down," she said.

I lowered into the chair, but no longer tried to get comfortable.

Taking a sip of her new drink, she seemed to make a decision. "You have a twin. So do I. So did your father."

"Okay." I raised my cup to my lips.

She took a deep breath. "So does everyone else on Golvern."

I spit the drink back into the cup. "A planet... of twins?"

"Many of our people settled on Earth over the years. They found life expectancy short because of your sun, but they also found humans were resilient. By mating with humans, their children inherited the same protections. Now twins are spread across Earth, but they are many generations removed, to the point that little or no power remains in their gene pool."

"Everyone on your planet has a twin?" I went over the conversation with Mom and Dad in my head, picking out the details. How did they—

Evelyn leaned over her cup. "There are exceptions to every rule."

I considered her words. "Why would anyone go to Earth knowing they would die early?"

"For freedom," Chase said.

Her shoulders sagged. "Those without a twin are treated unequal. In a way, our people are no better than those of this planet."

"Let me guess," I said, with a laugh. "People without a twin are forced to live separately without the same rights."

She looked at Chase. "What have you told her?"

"Nothing about the Lucha Noir," Chase said, crossing his arms.

"Who are the Lucha Noir?"

They both looked at me, but only Chase spoke. "The Lucha Noir fight for independence for all Singles. That's what we call people with no twin, or do you already know that?"

"I've never heard the name Lucha Noir before tonight."

"To us it means dark fighters," Evelyn said, reaching for a tablet at the edge of her desk. She used the thin metal device to fan her face. "Their last known leader disappeared twelve years ago. No one knows what happened to him. Rumors flow rampant across the stars, but most agree the group dissolved after his death. The remaining members fled underground, scheming and waiting patiently for their time to rise again."

I turned to Chase. "Can someone really disappear with all the technology you have?"

He grinned. "All the technology makes it easier than you think."

"Their leader was cold and calculating in battle," Evelyn said. "He covered his tracks well. The only thing we know for sure is his name."

"Which is?"

She stopped fanning her face and stared at me. Sweat trickled down her cheek. "Justin Delaney."

* * * * *

Dad was a dark fighter? I thought of the night Mom held the shotgun to Ronald's head and laughed. Yeah, he'd taught me to shoot, but a fighter? I found it extremely hard to imagine Dad ever went into battle.

"I don't believe her," I said as I paced in front of Chase.

He sat on the steps of Marsha's house, now completely dark. "There's no doubt in her mind about who he is. What she's not sure of is why."

I didn't bother to ask when Marsha disappeared or if she'd ever return. It was enough they let me leave the ship to work through the storm brewing in my head. All those years, all the lies. Did my parents know the whole time? Did they help murder my father? "They always told me the Naples were my parents, until I remembered they weren't. Dad found dozens of doctors to help with my memory, but so far I can only remember that night."

"What happened after the ship landed?"

I stopped pacing and stared at Chase. "I thought you said the ship crashed."

"That's what Mom claims, but I'm not sure anymore."

I sat on the step next to Chase. "There was an argument. Someone fired a gun and I believe that man killed our father."

"What did he look like?"

"I only remember his eyes as he raised the gun. They were filled with a blackness that seemed like the worst kind of evil. Then I was covered in blood. I ran outside, through the woods, and into a road. Next thing I knew, a man almost ran me down with his truck."

"Justin Delaney," he said.

"Yeah. My dad… he can't be…" A horrible thought entered my head. "What about Mom?"

"Lorraine?" he asked softly.

Wiping the tears, I failed miserably at detaching myself from the people I knew of as my parents. Less than twenty-four hours had passed, and I already wished desperately for their arms to circle around me. Mom could make this nightmare fade like the night would soon.

"She might be normal," he said. "Lorraine Conners is the missing piece to this puzzle. Like Justin, she was born on Earth, but Mom has found no evidence to connect her with the Lucha Noir."

"Why does *our* mother hate the Lucha Noir?"

"About the time we turned five, our government

decided the Lucha Noir were far more dangerous than previously thought. A plan was formulated, in secrecy, to destroy their network. She believes our father left to warn them and has insisted for years they were responsible for his death."

"How would he know about a secret plan?" I asked.

"Our parents both worked for the government. They knew where and when the massacre would happen."

"I don't think they were trying to kill him. They were after me."

Chase gripped my shoulders. "What did you say?"

"The man with evil eyes… he was trying to shoot me that night. Our father pushed me out of the way and died instead."

"That man was not part of the Lucha Noir."

I shrugged off his grip. "How can you know that?"

"Trust me, Jes. The Lucha Noir would never hurt you."

His confidence didn't make me feel any better.

* * * * *

"Ready?" Chase asked as we stood before the door to Evelyn's office.

"No," I said.

He smiled and pressed the square handle. The door opened to a scene of Evelyn sitting behind her desk and Renora leaning across the polished surface, almost into her face.

"She must go back," Renora insisted.

"No," Evelyn said. "I cannot lose her again."

Renora lowered her voice. "I understand your

struggle, but you must make the logical choice, not the emotional one."

Evelyn raised her head. "Logical is my daughter never leaving my side."

Looking back at me, Renora's face remained neutral. "If she were my daughter, what course of action would you suggest?"

Evelyn's eyes darted across each item on the desk before she answered. "A search for the truth."

Renora nodded. "The only way to ensure Kayden's safety today, as well as tomorrow and the next day, is to deal with the problem at hand."

"What if they hurt Kayden?"

"If they planned such vulgar action, do you not think twelve years would have offered ample time?"

"Sometimes I hate when you are right." Looking over me, Evelyn nodded and addressed Renora. "You are dismissed. Make the arrangements."

"Understood." Renora turned and left the room.

"What's going on?" I asked.

"They're sending you back," Chase said.

"Back?" I asked, as the walls began to tighten around me. "To Credence?"

"Now you know the truth," Evelyn said. "You must confront your abductors so we can understand their motive."

"Wait," I said, backing away. "You want me to face my parents?"

Evelyn pressed her lips. "They raised you and we shall find out why."

"I don't like this," Chase said.

Evelyn folded her hands in her lap. "The preparations are underway. We will complete this mission within twenty-four hours and return home."

My head spun. She wanted me to go back. How could I face my parents knowing they took me from my family and hid the truth for twelve years? "What time is it?"

"Three-thirty in Credence," Chase said.

I rubbed my eyes. Had I really stayed up all night? "They'll be up. They'll know."

Chase put his hands on the desk and leaned across. "I'm going with her."

"Too dangerous," Evelyn said, her steely eyes boring into Chase.

"I won't let them take her again," he said.

More words flowed through the room, charged with a steady stream of anger, but I blocked out the meaning as my fear transformed into a bright star of hope. My parents—I could see them again, talk about everything. No matter how dangerous Evelyn or Chase suggested they were, Justin and Lorraine were still my parents. I sighed as the truth settled into my heart.

I would see them, then I'd ask why... they would tell me or lie, oh god it didn't matter. Tears burst from my eyes. I covered my face with my hands. Mom's arms would be around me. Dad... I didn't care who he really was. Pade... I could see Pade again, and Bailey.

Feeling like such a jerk, I slapped at the tears under my eyes. I was crying for people who took me from my family and all I wanted was a few more hours with them. Through my glossy eyes, I noticed Chase and Evelyn's stares.

"Okay," I said, but the words didn't feel like mine.

"I'll help her get ready," Chase said, pulling me out of the door, but not before I felt the flay of pain from

Evelyn's eyes.

* * * * *

"What is she not saying?" I asked.

Chase guided me into a dark room and closed the door behind us.

"Lunas," he said.

I jumped as the room flooded with light. The first thing I noticed was the green comforter, almost the same shade as the one on my bed. "Is it cold in space?"

He grinned. "Nothing like New York."

"What is she not saying?" I asked again.

Chase crossed the room to sit in a desk chair, slowly as if gathering every additional second he could find before answering.

"How do you know so much about the Lucha Noir?" I asked.

"Do you trust me?"

"Yes." I took a seat on the bed.

He shifted in the chair, unable to get comfortable. "I joined the Lucha Noir."

I opened my mouth, but shock held me frozen as he stared.

"If you plan to turn me in, please do it now. I don't want to live in fear of *you* betraying me."

"I'll never turn you in," I said, without hesitation.

His face relaxed, but only slightly.

A knot formed in my stomach. "Why would you join them?"

"By accident, last spring. Remember when I said I was in prison?"

I nodded.

"I guess in Earth terms, you could call me a hacker. Growing up on Golvern, I was never allowed access to a computer, and I never thought to question why. When the computer stuck me in Mom's class last year, I decided to learn enough about computers to make sure that never happened again."

"Hacking sounds pretty serious," I said. "Why go that far?"

"Our government takes a tough stance against people who try to expose their secrets. I wanted to know why. When I was busted, I'd covered my tracks so well only Mom knew who I was. She got me out and suppressed all of the files, but she has no idea I met someone there who brought me into the Lucha Noir. They needed my skills, and I couldn't hate the government more. No one knows but you."

Would the secrets ever stop? "Why are you telling me this?"

"There's so much I should tell you, but there isn't time. Before you go back, I want you to understand the Lucha Noir aren't what you think. They're not some horrible disease affecting our people. They want freedom, and who can argue that point?"

"Are my parents really involved in this?"

Chase raised an eyebrow.

"My parents on Earth. I can't forget twelve years in one night."

"There's no way for me to know for sure. The Lucha Noir work in secrecy. Most members at my level don't know if the person standing next to them is a supporter of the group. They follow the First Principle."

"Which means?"

"When discovered, they claim to work alone." He

cleared his throat. "Punishment should never involve family."

"So all of this might just be a story someone made up?"

Chase shook his head. "Mom's information is better than even she realizes. I'm not sure how she found out, but she was right about Justin Delaney. To the Lucha Noir, he's important."

"What if she catches you working with them?"

"She must turn me in. In history class, you completed a unit about George Washington. I was there that day."

I nodded.

"That's how the Lucha Noir see Justin Delaney—as the leader of their revolution. No one knows for sure if he's still alive, but if he is, I'd give anything to meet him."

Laughing, I laid back on the bed, staring up at the black glass. Would I ever get used to not seeing my reflection? "Ten thousand humans could have the name Justin Delaney. There are probably sixteen in Alabama."

He considered. "But how many are raising Kayden Draigon, the Honra Ril? If he's George Washington, you're the girl in that TV show who played a singer while trying to attend high school. I watched it when I first came to Earth. You must have seen it—no one ever seemed to recognize her."

I sat back up. He and Bailey were so alike. "That's a little old school."

"But in the show, she lived a double life. You're living a double life without even knowing."

"Yeah, but she was a famous rock star. I thought you said Honra Ril means leftover girl."

"To most of Golvern it does, but to the Lucha Noir, Honra means honored."

"So, I've gone from leftover to honored?" I laughed.

"Mom frowns at the term but, like you, she doesn't understand." He stood. "Dawn is coming. Your parents will be up soon."

"How do you know they haven't already discovered my bed empty?"

"Technology," he said. "They're still in bed."

"Are you watching my house?" I asked, feeling creeped out, but pushed the thought aside.

"No," he said, "we haven't approached the house for fear of alarming them. If they are who we think. Heat sensors can show us their location from above. Do you have the charm I gave you?"

I patted the golden 'K' that hung from my neck. "I'll never lose it."

"Good," he said. "There's a tracking device inside. Press it and I'll appear wherever you are within twenty seconds. Don't be scared."

"I'm not. They've never hurt me."

Chase nodded. "The ship should be above Credence by now. I'll take you back."

"No," I said. "I need the practice."

"Press the stone and I'll be there."

I nodded and closed my eyes, picturing myself back in my bed, under my green comforter.

CHAPTER THIRTEEN

Home Again

I woke to darkness, lying perfectly still as my eyes adjusted to the outline of the window. A surge of emotion sped through my veins, and I recognized it as happiness. I was home. For months, I'd thought of Chase, of when he might come back to take me home. But that ship in the sky wasn't home.

For an hour or more, I snuggled against the comforter, relishing the warmth of lying in my bed once more. The floor below me remained silent. Chase was right. The treasures on my dresser began to take form as light grew until the window glowed with the hazy orange of morning. My room looked exactly as when I left, only hours before. Somehow it felt like a year had passed.

Sleep came, but not as fast as I wished. My mind wandered through the night—our flight to New York City, the shock of standing in the Naples' house after imagining that visit for so many years, our talks on the ship. Chase's betrayal. Stunned at his confession, I wondered what could be so bad about life on Golvern to make him risk everything.

Hours passed as the nightmares showed no mercy.

When my eyes opened next, the clock by my bed showed two o'clock in the afternoon. I rubbed the sleep from my eyes, amazed since I'd never slept that late.

Yawning, I walked down the stairs. The smell of coffee penetrated the air, along with bacon probably cold in the fryer, both of which reminding me I would soon lose everything. Mom sat at the kitchen table, shelling peas she pulled from a brown paper bag. She tossed the peas into a stainless bowl and the empty shells into the trash can, which she'd moved next to the table. Dad flipped the newspaper in his hands to a new page.

As I stood in the doorway, staring at this perfect view of a happy family, an avalanche of feelings overwhelmed me.

Hate. How could they steal me away from my real family?

Shame. I felt real shame for not realizing they lied. Twelve whole years of lies.

Love. I wanted to hug them both and never leave.

Pain. Why did they do this to me?

Happiness. I could have my old life back. We could leave for Atlanta…

Guilt. What would Chase and Evelyn think about me wanting my old life back?

Betrayal. Did these people ever love me?

Fear. What if they tried to hurt me? No, they would never hurt me.

Confusion. What did all of this mean for my future? For our future?

Strength. I'd confront them. They'd tell me everything.

Weakness—

"You must have been tired to sleep so late," Dad said.

If he only knew. "I stayed up reading all night."

"Bailey's been over three times already," Mom said.

Fresh guilt grew inside as I thought of the night before. If I had not returned, what would Bailey be saying now? I took my usual spot at the table. Weakness won out. For now, I'd be me again, until I had the nerve to confront them. How long would Chase wait?

Dad glanced over me and lifted the folded section of comics that sat in front of him. Underneath the paper was a book, which he slid across the table as I dropped into the chair. It came to a stop next to my hand.

Stunned, I could only stare at the copy of *Pride and Prejudice* given to me almost a year ago.

"Where did you get that book?" he asked.

Pain caught in my throat. "You guys went through my stuff?"

"This morning," Mom said, "while you were sleeping. I wanted to know if you had any more of those articles about the Naples. I think it's about time we put the whole box in the shredder."

Did they know about last night? "Bailey found the box in the shed. It was an accident, but you know how Bailey insists on investigating everything. She brought the article to school, to convince me I'm not Jessica Naples."

"And just how did she figure that out?" Mom asked.

My stomach rumbled. "Not from me. She noticed a birthmark in the picture."

"Enough about the Naples," Dad said. "I'll ask

again. Where did you get the book?"

"I got it for a book report last fall."

His face tightened as he almost lost his patience. "Who gave it to you?"

"Mrs. Pearson."

Mom looked up from the peas. "Chase's mother?"

And mine, I wanted to say. "She accused me of cheating in her class. She gave me an F on a test but let me do the book report to make up the grade. I think she felt sorry for me after the wreck."

Dad narrowed his eyes and pointed at the book. "Mrs. Pearson *gave* you that book to read?"

"She *loaned* it to me for a book report but disappeared before I could give it back."

His voice was focused, with a dangerous glint. "Did you read the whole book?"

"Yes sir," I said.

He stood and reached for the book, opening to the first page. Pointing at the handwritten notes, he looked at me. "You read this?"

It was the perfect time for me to tell him the truth, ask the tough questions. I would start with—who was I kidding? "I couldn't understand the notes. She said it was an old style of English."

He frowned and sat back in his chair. "Did they ask for anything else before they left?"

Yeah, a sample of my DNA. "Anything like what?"

"Did they ask you to give them anything?"

"No," I lied.

"What were they doing in Credence?"

The smell of pound cake began to fill the air. I shrugged as my stomach rumbled again.

Dad's hand slammed against the table. His next

words came out in short bursts. "You will tell me what I want to know."

I tried to picture him as a dark fighter. Truthfully, I couldn't picture him fighting anyone. Was he really who Chase claimed and would he tell me the truth if I asked? "They were looking for a kidnapped girl from New York. They thought I might be her."

"Dear god," Mom whispered. "They told you that?" Her hands shook worse than my voice.

Thinking fast, I recalled the night they left. "I told them the truth about the Naples. They saw the articles online and realized I couldn't be her."

"You told them the whole story?" he asked, as the shock of my words played across his face.

"It was the only way to get them to leave me alone."

"Did they threaten you?" Dad asked.

"Why would they do that?" I asked.

Dad stared at me. For a second or maybe two, I thought he might give an honest answer.

Mom finished the last of the peas. "While all of this is interesting, we need to focus on your father's upcoming treatments. The hospital is ready for us."

Nodding, Dad pushed away from the table. "We'll have a good dinner tonight and first thing in the morning we'll get on the road."

"We *are* coming back to Credence, right?" I asked.

"Sure honey," Mom said in a tired voice. The stove buzzed and she collected the peas, placing the bowl on the counter as she removed the cake and turned off the oven.

Dad opened the porch door, as Danny and Collin burst through.

"We're leaving first thing tomorrow," Dad said.

"Go upstairs and start packing."

"What? You're giving us more than twenty minutes?" Danny blasted and swung around to face Dad. "No, we're going to the lake tomorrow. One last time—you both promised we could take Sam."

I hadn't noticed how tall the boys had grown in nearly a year until I watched Danny almost standing toe-to-toe with Dad.

Collin pushed himself between them. "Dad's sick," he said to Danny. "Fighting isn't right."

Danny balled his fists. "Making us move again isn't right."

"Danny Delaney," Mom said, rising from the table. "Take that back."

"No." Danny got in Dad's face. "First you make us move to every city in the U.S.A. so Jes can be safe. Safe from what? Those stupid reporters you talked about from New York?"

Dad took a step back. "Where did you hear that?"

"You think we don't listen to what happens around here?" Danny crossed his arms. "Oh, then you get sick and make us move again."

Mom placed the cake on the table and reached for Danny. "You know that's not fair."

He shrugged away. "We want to stay in Credence." Danny looked at Collin.

"He's right," Collin said. "You told us this would be the last move."

Danny lowered his voice. "If you don't let us stay we'll tell everyone the truth about Jes."

Mom's face was a mixture of pain and anger. "Why would you hurt your sister?"

"She's not our sister," Collin said. "We've

overheard enough to figure out who she really is. We know why you made us move all those times."

Dad's eyes were incredulous. "What do you plan to do?"

"Tell everyone about New York," Danny said.

This was my chance to sneak out of the room, but watching the boys fight with Dad felt normal. I needed normal after the last twenty-four hours. Reaching across the table, I grabbed a butter knife left from breakfast. I cut a slice of cake and stuffed a huge yellow bite into my mouth. Closing my eyes, I savored the sweetness. Mom had become quite an expert at making cakes over the last year, and I wouldn't let myself imagine a world without her in it.

Collin looked at the floor. "You don't want to push us. We'll really tell everyone about Jessica Naples."

"Oh yeah?" Dad asked. "Now she's Jessica Naples to you?"

"No," Collin said miserably.

Danny shoved his elbow into Collin's ribs. "We have proof."

I took a bite of the brown crust—my favorite part. "So does all of Credence High."

Danny's face fell. "You're lying."

"Nope," I said, licking my fingers. "Bailey took one of the articles to school and now everyone knows, including your friend Samuel Greene. I know for a fact his dad saw the picture of me."

Dad looked at Mom as she closed her eyes. "You said Jes had the article at school, but did I miss something? The whole school knows?"

"Yeah," I said. "You worried for all of those years, and I haven't noticed a single reporter knocking on the door."

"I'm sorry," Mom said. "I didn't want to worry you any more than necessary. Not when we were already leaving."

Dad gave Danny an uneasy look. "Would you really do that to your sister?"

"Look at what she's done to us all of these years," Danny said.

"Go to your room," Dad said. "Both of you."

"But…" Collin said.

Dad sighed. "As much as I hate to admit it, you're right. All of those years we moved for Jes and the two of you were dragged along for the ride. Change into some old clothes and we'll go fishing. Maybe Joel and Sam can meet us."

Danny stood in a stupor until Collin pushed him toward the stairs.

"Don't encourage them," Mom said.

Dad took her hand in his. "I don't approve of their methods, but they're right. I haven't been much of a father always putting Jes first."

"We do what we must," Mom said, but released his hand when she realized I still sat at the table.

"Hey." Bailey stepped through the open door and around Dad. "What's going on in here?" She scanned the kitchen until she saw me. "Please tell me you asked about the party."

"Party?" Dad asked.

"Terrance is having a birthday party," Bailey said. "Pade and I are going; he's driving. Jes got invited too."

Mom moved aside as Bailey passed. "Pade and Terrance made up?"

"Well, not exactly. We're still working on the

forgiveness part."

"Can I go?" I asked.

Dad looked to Mom and then at me. "I suppose if you can stay out of trouble. No reason you can't see your friends one last time."

Bailey spun around. "You say that like you're leaving for good."

"We'll be in Atlanta for a while," Dad said, not taking his eyes off me. "Make sure you have your phone. Call us if there's any trouble."

* * * * *

"Are you still mad at me?" Bailey asked. "Is that why you didn't answer any of my texts last night?"

I stared at the darkness outside of the jeep. "No."

Bailey stayed silent until we pulled into Terrance's driveway. "I hope Angel comes tonight. She needs an intervention."

"What's wrong with Angel?" Pade asked, glancing in the mirror.

"She wants to break up with Skip. I told her she's an idiot."

"That makes no sense," Pade said. "Skip is totally in love with her. He never talks about anyone else."

"Angel doesn't agree, which is why she's an idiot."

"They'll both be here." He shook my arm. "You haven't said anything all night."

"I don't know where to start," I said, still staring out the window. How could I tell them about the night before? About seeing Chase? I felt along my shirt for the charm. Chase would be coming for me soon.

With Pade by my side, I wasn't so sure about going

back to Golvern. Yes, I wanted to know my mother. Yes, I needed Chase in my life. But going to New York had changed how I felt about my past in so many ways. I wanted to be me, and I wasn't sure if that included being Kayden.

"Did I do something wrong?" he asked, his voice serious. "You've been avoiding me all week."

The look on his face—it was time to tell him how I really felt. Before I missed my chance. "I've been trying to process Dad being sick again." I swallowed. "Pade, I want to–" I jumped when someone hit my window.

Skip laughed outside the glass. He opened the door and I noticed Angel standing to his side in a dark red sweater. Reaching for my hand, he helped me out of the jeep and then reached to help Bailey.

When Skip circled the jeep to talk with Pade, Angel held out her hand. On her fourth finger glimmered a tiny gold ring. "Skip promised we'd always be together." She smiled as Skip waved to her and followed Pade into the house. "Waiting is the right thing."

Bailey put her hands on her hips. "That's what I've been telling you."

"He loves me," Angel said, with a shining smile that matched her ring.

"Of course he does." Bailey threw an arm around her neck. "Now if I could only get my brother to understand that about Jes." She looked at me. "You were about to tell him, weren't you?"

My smile grew with the sadness I felt. "Yes."

"You'll get your chance," she said.

If my time didn't run out.

CHAPTER FOURTEEN

The Party

An hour later, Pade and Skip laughed outside on the wooden deck. I watched through the sliding glass door as Bailey and I stood in a dark corner of a living room with white and gold furniture that rarely saw visitors. Every time the speakers boomed, the cabinet of hand-blown glass rattled to my side. Terrance came to the door twice and looked out at Pade, but finally turned and disappeared back into the crowded kitchen.

"This party sucks," Bailey yelled.

I took a sip of the drink in my hand, focusing on the previous night. At first I thought the party would be a way to forget everything from the night before. But as I watched Pade, I realized there was nothing about the last twenty-four hours I could afford to forget. My whole world would soon change. Pade would know the truth about me, and Bailey. Or I'd disappear and they'd never know.

Thinking about Mom, I took another sip. I still doubted Dad's involvement even after Chase insisted, but was Mom really as innocent as he suggested? What did she know about me? Did she have a power?

Rachelle appeared at my side. "Can we go outside and talk?"

"What's going on?" Bailey asked.

"Nothing," I said, trying to remember if I'd told her about Rachelle's betrayal. No, that was another thing lost since yesterday. I looked over the deck where Angel had joined Skip. "Let's go out the front door."

Bailey finished her can of coke. "You go ahead, I've got to find the bathroom."

"I'm sorry," Rachelle said, the minute we stepped outside.

"For setting me up with Brianna?" I asked.

"No," said Brianna, who stepped out of the shadow of Skip's red truck. "For this." She grabbed one of my arms as Ronald jumped out from behind the truck to grab my other.

"What do you want?" I asked, trying to wrench at least one of my arms free.

"Payback," Ronald said. "For what you did to me in the hall. For making me think I'm crazy. We're going around back and you're going to show everyone what you can do."

I looked at Rachelle, who cowered a few feet away. "Why are you doing this to me?"

"I'm not the person you think I am," Rachelle said.

"Well," I said, "I can see that. Why set me up twice?"

"To make things right," she said.

"To make what right?" I asked. "Is this about Leigh Ann?" I turned to Brianna. "What have I done to you?"

She used the dainty voice again, which made me

want to throw up. "Nothing but hurt Ronald. He's been there for me and I take anything against him personal."

"I didn't hurt Ronald," I said. "He came after me."

"You got him suspended," Brianna said. "He only pulled that alarm because I asked him to."

Okay, maybe if I played her game they'd let me go. No way could I show my power here. "Why did you ask him?"

Brianna smiled. "To prove he cared."

Calling her motive dumb might not get the job done. "I can see he cares about you."

"He does," she said, giggling. "He's the only one who's been there for me since…" Her face fell. "Leigh Ann was my sister, until someone at school found out about them." She pointed to Rachelle. "They threatened to post the picture everywhere. That's why Leigh Ann…" Sobs followed the horrible cry uttered with the name.

Ronald released my arm to wrap his around Brianna. "It's okay."

"It's my fault," Rachelle said. "I didn't know Leigh Ann wasn't strong enough to deal."

Brianna pulled away from Ronald. "Don't *you* say that about her. And you're right, this *is* all your fault." She put her hands on her hips and got in my face. "I demanded to quit that school my parents always insisted on. I wanted to come here and find the girl who destroyed my sister's life."

"I cared about Leigh Ann," Rachelle muttered.

"Not enough to save her." Brianna inched closer to my face.

I had the power to stop Brianna. I could blink myself away, but the look on Rachelle's face bothered me more than the tiny droplets that sputtered against my cheek as Brianna spoke. "I'm sorry for your loss."

"Sorry? *Sorry?* Is that all you've got?"

"No." I looked at Ronald. "You think I can do more, which could be bad for you. But I won't if we end this now."

"This will never be over," Brianna said.

"Until what?" I asked. "Until Rachelle is so tormented she kills *herself?* That won't make this better."

Brianna's face changed, to the point she looked close to tears. "I want her to feel what I lost."

"Doesn't she?" I asked.

Rachelle wiped the tears from her eyes. "Yes."

Backing away from Brianna, I put an arm around Rachelle's shoulders. "I was there the day she got the news. She cried on me for hours. If you think she hasn't suffered, you're wrong."

"But what you did to Ronald—"

"I didn't want to turn him in, but Dr. Greene showed up as he ran off and I didn't have any choice. I considered telling him I did it, but he never would have believed me."

"You would have taken the hit?" Ronald asked.

"Yes," I said. "I don't like ratting people out. But Mom showed up and I was stuck."

Brianna looked from Ronald to me. "You still need to explain yourself. What Ronald said happened in the hall…"

"It wasn't me," I lied. "It was the guy with me. Joe."

"Your imaginary friend?" Rachelle asked.

"No," Ronald said. "He was there. Maybe…" He slapped a palm to the side of his head. "Maybe I am going crazy."

"You're not crazy, Ronnie." Brianna circled her arms around him.

Ronald and Brianna—they were made for each other. Seeing my opportunity, I ran back to the living room, pushing through the crowd of laughter and dancing. Rachelle's eyes followed me, but I didn't have time to sort out how I felt about her. It was time to find Bailey and get out of there before Brianna changed her mind.

Out on the deck, Skip spun Angel as they danced. Pade was nowhere to be seen.

I walked through the kitchen, slamming into Tosh. The drink in her hand crashed against the floor and splashed in every direction. "Sorry," I said.

"Don't worry about it." She reached for a roll of paper towels.

"Have you seen Bailey?" I asked. "Or Pade?"

"Pade went upstairs to Terrance's room. They're supposed to be talking, but I haven't heard anything break yet."

I peeked in each of the three bedrooms but no Pade. The last door was closed. I hesitated to knock long enough for the door to open, leaving Pade to stare at me.

He reached for my hand, pulled me around the door, and slammed it behind me. We were alone in the room, our only light a dim lamp next to the bed. "I thought you were Terrance, but I'm glad you're not."

Pade leaned in and kissed me softly as he wrapped his arms around me. "I've dreamed about us being alone again, but that never seems to happen."

"You've got me now," I said.

His eyes grew with the realization this was our

chance. He locked the door behind me and took my hand in his. "I'm never letting you go." Kissing me deeper, he moaned as I pulled him closer.

The alcohol on his breath stung my nose and tasted like a mixture of honey and tar.

"We could leave town tonight, just you and me," he said. "I'll be eighteen in two months."

I smiled. A thousand reasons that couldn't happen zipped through my head, but I dismissed every one. The only thing that mattered to me was his lips against mine. I loved Pade—I'd never stopped, though my feelings were so different from a year ago.

He led me to the bed, lowering me on top of the white and navy bedspread. Reaching to both sides of my face, he spread my hair to fan out around me. "You look like an angel."

His laughter felt like a giddy comedy routine, but it was the first time he'd laughed like that since Colorado. The music around us faded as we entered our own world, one with sunflower fields to the edge of sight, where we could run for hours. A daring thought entered my mind. "Let's make tonight special."

The laughter stopped as Pade's expression grew serious. He sat on the bed next to me, reaching down to kiss me with a gentleness that brought tears to my eyes. "Tonight is already special," he whispered.

Deeper he kissed me, drawing me closer as he snuggled into the bed beside me. One of his hands slid along my cheek, while the other gripped my hand. "I love you."

"Me too," I whispered.

Pade pulled back and stared into my eyes. "I think you really mean it," he said, his voice as silky as my favorite chocolate.

A banging sounded on the door. The handle shook, followed by Terrance's voice.

"Damn," Pade said.

I laughed. "You said this never seems to happen."

He smiled. "It was enough to see you look at me like that."

The door rattled again. Pade gave me a quick kiss and jumped from the bed. As soon as the door opened, Terrance pulled Pade into the hall.

I scrambled from the bed and into the hall, in time to see Terrance throw a fist at Pade's face.

Pade fell to the floor, cradling his cheek. "Damn it," he said, spitting blood onto the hardwood floor.

The bathroom door opened beside me and Bailey stepped into the hall, holding Chase's hand.

"What are you doing here?" I asked.

"Making up for the last year," Chase said, his eyes watery.

Bailey wiped the smear of lipstick from the corner of Chase's mouth. "He came back to me."

Pade looked up at Chase. "Where the hell did you come from?"

"Let's take this outside," Terrance said.

"What did I do now?" Pade asked.

"Mia broke up with me, because of you."

"You're crazy." Pade lunged at Terrance.

Pade and Terrance rolled across the floor, punching at anything they could hit. Pade slammed an elbow into Terrance's head. Terrance kicked Pade in the stomach and broke away, climbing to his feet.

Doubling over in pain, Pade looked up at Terrance. "Hasn't this gone on long enough?"

"I thought we could talk." Terrance pointed at me. "You come to my party and end up on my bed with your bitch."

"She's not in this." Pade lunged again. The crowd of onlookers separated as the pair went head-first down the stairs.

"Pade," I screamed and raced Bailey down the stairs.

"Hey," someone yelled, "the parents are home."

In the midst of people running for the doors, Bailey managed to help Pade up, and I followed them to the jeep.

Pade pulled a set of keys from his pocket. The keys fell from his hand and he reached out, but lost his footing and fell to his knees. Cursing, he raked his hands through the grass around him.

"You can't drive," Bailey said. "You've had way too much to drink."

"I haven't," Pade said, but his words ran together.

"Can you drive the jeep?" I asked Bailey.

"She doesn't have a license," Pade whined.

Bailey looked back at the door. "What the hell?"

Chase was crossing the yard with Tosh in tow. "I've got a better idea."

Tosh pulled two keys on a tiny ring from her pocket, dangling them in front of Bailey. "I can drive a stick. Take my car."

Chase reached down and retrieved the keys from the grass next to Pade, as if he knew exactly where the keys had fallen. "Here," he said, handing the keys to Tosh. "Take the jeep and don't stop until you get to the rest area in Georgia. I've got someone set up to take you from there."

"What are you talking about?" I asked Chase.

"My escape," Tosh said, gripping the keys to her chest. Her face glowed with a happiness I never knew she possessed. "Chase promised to get me and my mom out of town."

"I said I'd help you," Pade moaned, his head hung low. "Why does *he* have to save you?"

Tosh lowered to her knees beside Pade. "You've already been a better friend to me than anyone, anywhere. You were willing to protect me when no one else cared. You helped me and all I did was lie to you."

"Lie?" Pade asked, his head snapping to attention.

"Yes," Tosh said, smiling sadly. She took his hand in hers. "I'm not pregnant. My step-dad didn't rape me. He did beat up on my mom, and the police know his record, but he never touched me like that. It was the only thing I could say to get Mom out of his house."

"You really made up being raped?" Bailey asked, a look of pity on her face.

Tosh nodded. "You don't know what it's like to be a prisoner in your own house."

"Oh, yes I do," Bailey said.

Chase gripped Bailey's arms, turning her to look into his eyes. "I've been back for weeks. I overheard Tosh's problems and promised to help her disappear."

"Why didn't you find me before?" she asked.

"I wasn't coming back to stay. But then I saw you tonight and I knew if we didn't talk, I might never have another chance."

A siren sounded in the distance, first as a low whistle, then as a force of power gaining momentum over the wind.

"Go time." Tosh turned to me. "Good luck."

I wondered if she knew where Chase would take me next.

Chase reached for Pade's arm, pulling him up to stand, but Pade shrugged him off. Bailey raced for the driver's door of the white car. I walked beside Pade to the car, barely noticing as Tosh drove off in the jeep. Chase climbed into the passenger seat next to Bailey.

"Want me to drive?" Chase asked as I climbed in behind him.

Bailey turned the key. "Have you ever driven a car?"

"Not exactly," Chase said with a smile. "But it can't be harder than flying."

Pade stopped next to Bailey's window. "He's not going with us."

"Get in," Bailey said, "or get your ass left."

I leaned across the seat and opened the door. "Please."

Pade said a few words I couldn't hear and dropped into the seat next to me, closing the door as Bailey backed the car out of the driveway and spun tires. She floored the accelerator.

"Yeah," Pade grumbled, "tear it up." He looked at me. "Are you going to argue with me about Chase too?"

How could I tell Pade who Chase really was? He'd think I was crazy. "He can help us."

"Sure he can," Pade said. "So, sister dear, what is so important about Chase? Why did we have to bring him?"

Bailey's eyes didn't leave the road. "That's none of your business. Besides, what did Chase ever do to you?"

Pade laughed, an annoying cynical sound. "Come on, Sis. You can't still like Chase after all this time. What does your best friend think about you and Chase?"

"What does that matter?" I asked.

The alcohol on Pade's breath filled the air between us. "Well, you like him don't you?" He laughed again, but with no semblance of humor. "Remember you talked about the guy you loved? The one who left? You see, Jes, I always listen to what you say. Only one guy left you and that's Chase Pearson."

Bailey glanced over her shoulder, enough for me to see the furor in her eyes. "You are the biggest idiot I've ever met, Pade Sanders." She drove the car off the road and into the dirt, slamming into park. She flung herself around to look into her brother's eyes. "She was talking about you!"

The color drained from Pade's face. "You were in love with me the whole time?"

I wanted to laugh at his pitiful sound, but I'd had enough drama for one night. "That's kind of hard to say at the moment."

"What about Chase?" His eyes pleaded. "Why did he come back?"

"Because," I said, "he's my brother."

"What?" Bailey cut her eyes to Chase.

"Yes," Chase said. "Jes is the sister I lost at five. My twin."

Bailey looked from Chase to me to Pade, then back at me. "He's your brother? I mean, your real life honest to god blood brother? That's what Chase meant, right? About you being his twin?" She shook her head in disbelief. "And he's from Golvern. That means…"

The air inside the car felt stale. "So am I."

She shook her head again, but next to me Pade's eyes were fixed straight ahead. "There's something I should tell you. Pade and I…"

Before she could finish, a light from behind flashed inside the car. The glow gave shadows to Pade's face that made me sick inside.

"There's someone coming up from behind," Bailey said as the car slowed to a stop behind us. "I'm getting us out of here." She threw the car into gear and pulled back onto the road in a storm of dust.

"Faster," Chase said, craning his neck to see the car.

"Oh my god," Bailey screamed. "They're going to hit us!"

In the next seconds, we were slammed from behind twice. "Pade," Bailey screamed, "what do I do?" The car pulled up close and slammed us a third time. She almost lost control but swerved to hold her place on the dark road. "Jes, call someone! Call 911!" She slowed around a curve, taking us around the edge of Lake Credence.

"Can't you drive faster?" Pade asked, as if just grasping we were in danger.

"The authorities can't help us," Chase said, his voice rattled. "They're after me and Jes."

I closed my eyes and pictured myself outside of the car. No, I couldn't leave everyone. As the car swerved again, I opened my eyes and stared at Chase, silently willing him to do something to save us. I wasn't strong enough yet. He'd have to overcome his fear.

His eyes met mine. Chase knew what I was thinking, but instead of saving us, he covered his face with his hands. "I can't..."

"Can't what?" Bailey asked. "Why would—?" she started, but a fourth hit was more than she could handle. The car left the road and rocketed down a slope. Through grass almost as tall as the car and branches that seemed to reach out in warning we crashed, our dim headlights illuminating only a few feet in front of us. The car fishtailed and turned over, gaining speed as if carried by a river rushing toward massive falls. My last vision was of a final crash, where the remaining light caused an explosion of sparkles in my eyes.

* * * * *

Sitting upside down, held only by a seatbelt that sliced into my shoulder, I came to the conclusion I really didn't like Tosh. And I definitely didn't want to die in her car.

Gravity pulling against me in the darkness didn't help the situation. I tapped the glass to my right and ran my hand below the bottom edge of the window. Gripping the window handle, I said a silent thanks that Tosh's car had the old-style manual roll-down windows. Maybe if I could get the window down, I could climb out. I didn't expect the rush of cold water that spilled through the gap.

As I fought to turn the handle back and stop the water, I noticed my cell phone, still gripped tight in my left hand. I'd pulled it out to dial 911. I pressed a button and a beacon of light radiated the backseat. Pade was still next to me. Thankfully, even in his drunken state he'd chosen to strap on the seatbelt. When I shoved his arm, he slowly opened his eyes.

"What happened?" he asked.

"We crashed into the lake. We're upside down in the water."

With my cellular flashlight, I could see that Bailey and Chase were deathly still. Both airbags in the front had deployed, and I prayed that one safety was enough. Pade hit both seats from behind, while yelling Bailey's name, but neither she nor Chase stirred.

In my mind, I covered the short list of possible ways for us to escape. Pade was drunk, upset, and trying to recover his bearings. Although I knew he couldn't be much help, I clutched his hand when the car lurched as if he could keep me from falling.

"We're filling with water," Pade said, his voice sobering fast.

There was only one way out, and unfortunately, I'd have to make three trips. Would I still have power left after one trip? My stomach twisted, for I wasn't even sure I could move an entire person. I wondered what Pade would say. "I can get me and one other person out."

"How do you plan to do that?"

The car lurched again. "It's hard for me to explain, but—"

"There's no time. You get Chase and I'll get Bailey." With those words, he placed a hand on Bailey's shoulder and I did the same for Chase. I closed my eyes and pictured the two of us on the lake's shore. *Please don't be upside down,* was my last thought. When I looked down, I was on my knees with Chase lying in front of me, stretched out across the ground. He moaned but didn't open his eyes.

A noise sounded behind us and I turned to see Pade on his knees next to Bailey. When I saw her move, I released the breath I'd been holding.

"What happened?" she asked as Pade helped her to sit upright.

"We crashed into the lake," he said.

"How did we get out?" Bailey's eyes focused on Chase and then on me. "There's no way you got us all out, not in your state."

"No," Pade said. "I got you out and Jes got Chase out." His eyes landed on mine, searching my soul as if meeting me for the first time.

"Jes?" Bailey shook her head. "She really does have a power, like us?"

Pade's eyes didn't leave me. "Apparently so."

The peculiar blend of shock and pain in Pade's voice tore at my insides. I turned back to Chase, unable to think of anything intelligent to say. Pade helped Bailey to her feet and they approached, each stopping to kneel on one side of me. Questions? Boy, did I have enough for the rest of the night.

"Is he okay?" Bailey whispered.

"I don't know," I said, leaning down to hear the words forming on Chase's lips.

"Call… your mom."

"Evelyn?" I asked. "You want me to press the charm?"

"No," he said, his voice ragged, "call Lorraine." It took every bit of energy for Chase to form the next words. "She's a Protector. She… will help… us."

Bailey exchanged a troubled glance with Pade. I dialed Mom's number and she answered after only two rings.

"Jes," she said, "is everything okay?"

"Nothing is okay," I said.

Her voice filled with urgency. "Where are you?"

"We went off the road into Lake Credence. The last turn in the road near the lake. Mom?"

"Yes?" she asked.

"Chase is with us and he's hurt. Please come now."

The call ended and all I could do was stare at the

tiny light that disappeared five seconds later. My hands shook as I considered redialing, but my fingers wouldn't cooperate. In less than a minute, I heard a noise above us on the hillside. Mom and Dad were making their way through the bushes.

"Jes!"

"Down here," I yelled, my voice shaking. They were really here. They'd really zapped themselves here to help us.

Dad rushed to my side, but Mom didn't bother to run. Instead, she appeared on the other side of Chase.

"Are you okay?" Mom asked.

I shook my head. "Just help Chase. Please," I begged as the tears began to sting my eyes. I no longer had to be strong. "Don't let him die."

Mom took Chase's head in her hands. "We need Charlie." She looked at Pade. "Call your mother and tell her to come now."

Pade's eyes were cloudy, maybe because of the alcohol. He turned and dialed his phone. Before I could look back up, Aunt Charlie stood next to Mom.

"Someone tried to kill us," Bailey said.

"Who?" Dad asked, alarm taking over his voice.

"We don't know," she said with a shiver. "Chase thought they were following him."

"They ran us off the road," Pade said.

"In the jeep?" Aunt Charlie asked.

"No," Bailey said. "We were in Tosh's car."

"That girl?" Aunt Charlie reached for Pade's arm, but he took a few steps back. "Look, no one really thinks… why not admit that silliness about Tosh is a lie?"

"It is a lie. Why didn't you ask before you called

Dad?"

She shortened the gap between them. "Pade Sanders, have you been drinking?"

Pade looked at the ground.

Aunt Charlie grabbed his arm, shaking as if trying to force him back to reality. "Don't tell me you were drinking and driving."

"I drove," Bailey said, "which is why we took Tosh's car. And no, I haven't been drinking."

"Charlie, not now," Mom said. "We've got to get Chase to a hospital."

Dad scanned the trees around us. "Credence Memorial will have to do for the moment. I don't see anyone, but we should hurry. Most likely whoever ran you off the road was the first contact. The second will come ready for combat."

Mom looked me over carefully. "What has Chase told you?"

Tears slipped down my cheeks and I wiped them away. "He said to call you. He said you would help because you're a Protector."

Mom's eyes glossed and Dad looked away. "Yes, that I am. Did Chase tell you why he came back?"

"He came back for me," I said.

"But why?" Dad asked.

How many times would I say the words before they felt real? "Because he's my brother."

Dad stood, unable to meet my eyes. "Did he take you anywhere?"

"To New York," I said, "last night. I got to meet Marsha Naples. And see my real mother again."

"Oh honey," Mom said. "Then you know about everything."

"No," I said, "none of this makes any sense. Chase said you're a Protector. But who are you protecting?"

Mom opened her mouth, but Dad said the words. "She's protecting you."

CHAPTER FIFTEEN

The Reasons Why

Aunt Charlie got us through the waiting room at Credence Memorial and back to see a doctor in less than five minutes, which I never imagined was possible. Mom and Dad followed close behind the bed holding Chase, through the main locking doors and into the triage area. We found a waiting room with one table of magazines and half a dozen chairs. Three chairs sat to one side of the small table, facing three chairs to the other.

Bailey and Pade decided to walk to the cafeteria, insisting on finding a drink machine.

"Don't go far," Aunt Charlie warned. "We might need to leave at a moment's notice."

Pade rolled his eyes as he and Bailey started down the hall.

I watched Mom and Dad from the doorway of the waiting room but couldn't bring myself to stand near the window separating them from Chase.

"They're doing everything they can," Aunt Charlie said.

My hands shook. "I know."

She gripped one of my hands. "Be strong for him."

"I can't lose him again," I said, on the verge of tears.

"I'm going to check on the boys." Aunt Charlie placed a hand on my shoulder. "This isn't the time for tears, my dear. Fate is on our side, but *you* must not lose hope. Then all would be lost." She took a quick glance around and then disappeared.

"Won't the cameras see her?" I asked as Mom walked up.

"We'll be gone long before anyone notices a blip on a screen in that security office. Charlie says the night guards have a habit of dozing off after ten."

Dad followed her into the room. He held a device in his hand—Chase's phone. "How much do you want to bet this has a tracking device?"

I pulled the necklace from under my shirt. "Chase said this is a tracking device. He wanted me to press the stone if anything bad happened."

"It's only a matter of time then," Dad said.

Mom fingered the charm and sighed. The charm disappeared, leaving only the gold chain to fall against my shirt. "That should throw them off." She dropped into one of the chairs and leaned her head back, closing her eyes.

"Speaking of time…" Dad said, his voice trailing off. He straightened and stared beyond the doorway as if a ghost had entered the hall.

"Who are you looking for?" someone asked from the hall.

"My son," said a familiar voice.

I leaned around the door to see Evelyn standing

next to a nurse. The nurse regarded the two men in black suits over her glasses, which slid halfway down her nose. "They can't be in here."

Evelyn motioned to the men, who retreated beyond the locking doors in the hall.

"You say he's your son?" the nurse asked, skeptical. "What about the people who brought him in?"

"Family friends," Dad said, pushing me behind the door. He stepped into the hall as I inched from behind the door enough to see her.

"You," Evelyn said, her words a cold command. She walked calmly to stand before Dad, her eyes locking with his, her expression unreadable. "You are Justin Delaney?"

"Who I am is not important." He backed away.

She moved closer, her voice rising with every word until she stood in the waiting room doorway. "You are the man who kept my daughter from me for twelve years?"

"Kayden needed our protection."

The room spun. I struggled to breathe. In my heart, I'd hoped to be wrong about him, but he'd known my real name all along. There was no longer any question in my mind. He must be the dark fighter Chase admired.

Evelyn regarded Mom warily. "Lorraine Conners."

Mom nodded but didn't meet her searching eyes. "I am Lorraine, daughter of Candorice Conners, formerly Candorice Reisten of Golvern."

"You had a twin?" Evelyn asked.

"She died when I was five. My mother was a Protector and I am beneficiary of her legacy. My sworn duty for the last twelve years has been to serve and protect Kayden."

"And your involvement with the Lucha Noir?" Evelyn asked.

Mom shifted in her seat and shot Dad an alarmed look. Slowly, she raised her eyes to meet Evelyn's. "Please don't hurt my children. The secrets I've kept became mine before they were born."

Evelyn faced Dad again. "I have been told Justin Delaney was the leader of the Lucha Noir before his disappearance."

Dad crossed his arms. "You have been told correctly. I'm still their leader."

"Then you uphold what they fight for."

"With every thread of my being."

"We never meant to keep Kayden from you all of these years," Mom said. "But whoever hurt Chase is after her."

"I know." Evelyn lowered her head.

The nurse from the hall entered the room, along with a doctor.

"Your son is stable for now," the doctor said, "but we need to do an MRI. You can see him."

Evelyn nodded, seeming to struggle for words.

"He'll be okay?" Dad asked.

The doctor turned to Dad. "He may have a concussion, but we need to get the results to know for sure."

"I will follow in a moment," Evelyn said and the doctor nodded. As he left the room, Evelyn looked at Mom. The power in her voice returned. "We are not finished yet. I want to know more about why this happened. I want to understand why you took my daughter." Her eyes narrowed. "You will not lie to me. You know who I am."

Mom bowed her head slightly. "Yes, your Highness."

"Whoa," I said, my head spinning. It wasn't the room. We were in a freaking movie. "What did you call her?"

Dad chuckled, but his voice held more of a 'told you so' sound. "It seems she left something out."

I crossed the floor to stand before her. "Chase said you work for the government."

"In a commanding role," she said.

"That's what you were taking me back to?" I asked. "Oh my god, no."

"I have no choice," Evelyn said quietly. "When your father left, I had to take his place. Then he died, leaving me alone."

"Kayden suffered a trauma that night," Dad said. "Her memory has never returned. We've exhausted every resource in our effort to unlock it."

"She does not remember me." Evelyn pursed her lips. "Or her father."

"Can we talk to her?" Dad asked, jamming his hands in his pockets. "At least have the opportunity to explain the last twelve years?"

"Yes," she said, "but you will answer to me after I see my son. You will not leave this place with her."

"Agreed," Dad said, his voice filled with resignation.

Evelyn took a long look at me and left the room.

Mom reached for my hand, but I pulled away. Dad sat beside her while I took a seat across from them. A cup of coffee appeared in Dad's hand. He offered it to Mom, but she shook her head. He placed it on the table.

"Do you think Chase will be okay?" I asked.

"I hope so," Dad said.

"Can I see him?"

"After we talk."

Silence filled the room as I considered where to start a million questions.

"Jes," Mom said, "we deserve the chance to tell our side."

I crossed my arms. "My name is not Jes, or Jessica, or anything resembling what you've called me for the last twelve years. And you knew the whole time."

Dad sighed. "Okay, Kayden. Does that make you feel better?"

I shrank from his words. His voice held a bitter edge that seemed unfair at the least. "None of this makes me feel better. Last night I found out the two people who raised me..." I swallowed hard. "You guys kidnapped me?"

Dad stared at me strangely. "After everything, you still don't remember that night?"

"No," I whispered as the tears started to fall. "I remember getting on the ship. I remember a man with a gun. After that, I only remember running through the woods and the headlights."

Mom clenched her fists. Pain burned in her eyes.

I wanted to hate them. I *needed* to hate them, desperately. These people took my life away. The tears became a river.

Mom shook her head and leaned forward, opening her arms.

Guilt bubbled in my throat, welling up to mix with the tears. How had my almost normal life become this?

I stood, willing my feet to run away from her arms. Her eyes met mine and I could see her love for me shining through her tears. I reached for her embrace, landing in her lap as my whole body shook.

"Honey," she said, smoothing my hair. "In no way did we kidnap you. No one kidnapped you. You hid on your father's ship. When he realized, you were past the point of no return."

"I saw the man with the gun. He shot... my real father." I swatted the tears, picturing the evil face looking down at me as the bullet exploded, and felt my father's arms shove me from the bullet's path. I turned to Dad. "Please tell me you weren't involved with killing him."

"I didn't kill anyone that night," Dad said, "although the thought did cross my mind after the gun went off."

"I understand now," I said. "My father tried to protect me, but the evil man shot him."

Dad gripped my hand, a look of pity in his eyes. "You remember him dying?"

I pulled my hand away and held it up. "There was blood on my hands, my face." I touched my cheeks.

Mom hugged me tighter. "You don't have to remember."

"He died saving my life. I need to remember." I looked at Dad. "You were there." I spun around to face Mom. "And you."

"Yes," Mom said, so quietly I wouldn't have heard her words had I not been sitting on her lap.

Dad nodded. "After he... your father died, others would have come for you. Dangerous others. We knew you must be protected."

"Where were we?" I asked.

"We were in an old farmhouse," Dad said, "outside

of New York City. There was an argument over—"

"Me," I said.

"Yes," Dad said. "After the gun went off, you ran from the farmhouse and into the woods. You'd never seen snow, but that didn't keep you from racing through the night."

Mom released my arms. "Justin had a truck—the old Ford, you remember?"

"I jumped in," Dad said. "I didn't think, just turned the key and hit the gas. I knew your feet were bare and you wouldn't get far. It wasn't long before I found you, teeth chattering, but you wouldn't speak. It was a month before you uttered another word."

"Lorraine washed the blood off your hands." He put an arm around Mom's neck. "I'm so sorry," he mumbled as he kissed her forehead.

"We called you Kay Ray," Mom said, with a sorrow deeper than I ever remembered. "We tried everything to make you remember, but somehow you blocked out that night, along with everything before it. We still don't know why you screamed whenever you saw water."

"Chase," I said. "He was in the water beneath the platform as I snuck onto the ship. I thought he drowned that night. He said our aunt kidnapped him, but our mother saved him. I didn't remember him in the water until the night before my last birthday."

"You blocked it out," Dad said, unable to hide the pain that coursed through his voice. "Your mother would've come for you too. I knew she couldn't keep you safe, not after that night."

"Justin and your father were friends," Mom said. "Your father came to Earth to warn our team about a pending strike."

"Either of us would have died to save your life. All he wanted was to save others. He never planned to involve you." Dad smiled, which appeared as more of a strain on his lips than anything. "Is there anything else you'd like to know?"

Yeah, twelve years' worth of truth. "Why make me think I was really Jessica Naples?"

"Justin and I had a past, a life on Earth," Mom said. "If we wanted to hide you here on Earth, you needed a past too. Authorities don't take kindly to people who appear with no birth certificate or social security number."

"Does that really happen?" I asked.

She laughed as if she'd never been so tired. "Haven't you ever read one of those tabloids in line at the grocery store?"

"So, there we were," Dad said, "sitting in a coffee shop trying to get you to eat something when a picture of Jessica Naples came over the news. You remember, the one with the bear?"

I shivered. "How could I forget?"

Dad smiled. "I looked at Lorraine and asked, 'you thinking what I'm thinking?'"

His comical voice did nothing to make me feel better. "You decided based on one picture?"

Mom nodded. "It made sense at first. She was four—you'd just turned five. You were about the same height and size. We dyed your hair to make it brown like in her picture. She had blue eyes, so no problem there. Justin went to the police, claiming he'd found you. It really was the perfect lie. We tracked the Naples, and they'd already made it to Florida. They weren't coming back."

"Then the TVs caught on to the fact they were gone. No one could understand why they'd disappeared, when Marsha Naples had begged for her daughter's safe return, crying herself sick on camera only one week before."

"The reporters wanted to interview you," Mom said. "They wanted to take pictures of us."

"So, everyone just bought it? I find that hard to believe."

"It was a great story," Dad said, with sarcasm. "Girl from the gutter disappears, leaving the police convinced she'd never be found. Witnesses said her parents shot up with her there, but they didn't have enough evidence of wrongdoing. And worse, no one really cared. It was the perfect cover for you."

"What about fingerprints?" I asked.

Mom waved a hand. "Fingerprints are easy."

Dad sighed. "We all *needed* to disappear, but you can't hide in front of ten thousand cameras."

"Bailey's dad helped us," Mom said. "He had the means to get us out of New York. The story of your past couldn't change—we were kind of locked in at that point. You were really Jessica Naples. I kept the box of articles in case we ever needed to prove it."

"You'd go to that kind of trouble?" I asked. "It seems strange since all those years you insisted I *not* tell anyone about New York."

"Anything to keep you safe," Dad said. "We never lied about that fact. You being Jessica Naples kept the bad guys off your track."

"Who are the bad guys in this whole scenario?"

"Anyone wanting to keep you from saving the Lucha Noir." Mom stilled. "I'm assuming you've heard of them by now."

"According to Evelyn—"

"Evelyn?" Dad asked.

"That's what she told me to call her." I pulled myself from Mom's lap and once again sat across from them. "I had trouble calling her mom."

"She *is* your mother," Dad said. "You shouldn't feel guilty."

"But it's weird," I said. "I've always known you guys adopted me, but seeing her… it changes everything."

Mom leaned forward and rested her head on her hands. "What did she say about the Lucha Noir?"

"Basically, the same as your government lesson. About the planet with twins?"

"Nice touch, huh?" Dad's eyes gleamed. "You got the message, and with impressive perception. I don't think I've ever felt more pride than in that moment."

This man who raised me, lying to my face for years, still made my heart swell. He was the enemy. I was a horrible daughter. "She said you're their leader."

"Yes," Dad said.

"Chase thinks she's wrong, that the Lucha Noir are fighting to free people. There's another thing I want you to explain. He said the Lucha Noir call me Honra Ril. What does that mean to you?"

Dad's grin faded. "How would Chase know…" He looked at Mom, alarm growing on his face.

"Because he joined them," I said. "After he and Evelyn left last year, Chase became some kind of hacker and landed in jail. He said they needed his skills."

Amazement replaced the alarm. "Son of the queen of Golvern joining the Lucha Noir? Does she know?"

"No, but what did Mom mean about me saving the

Lucha Noir?"

"It's a rumor," Dad said. "We've lived on Earth for many years, far removed from the inner-workings of that planet. Years ago, someone got the bright idea you'd somehow help the Lucha Noir win their revolution. Our revolution. There are those who believe they can predict the future. We call them—"

"Olsandyols," I said.

"You always learned fast," Mom said, with a somber look. "The Olsandyol was careless in speaking those words, especially since you were so young. No one is sure of how or when, but the moment that prediction was made you became a target."

"Whenever we ran," Dad said, "it was because we felt someone was too close to the truth. That's why we never wanted you to talk about New York. We didn't need reporters showing up who might take a picture of us."

I shook my head. The story made perfect sense. After all, it sounded too convoluted to be fake. No wonder they'd made me lie, why they acted unhinged when I was barely twenty feet away. No wonder they'd been so worried about me. "If all of this is true, why did you guys let me go out? To the movies? To the game? Riding in the jeep?"

"Everywhere you went, Bailey and Pade were there," Mom said. "Even though they didn't know you were one of us, they knew how to contact us if anything happened. We couldn't exactly keep you locked in the house forever."

I thought of the day Pade seemed hesitant to take me to the airport. "Am I a danger to you?" I thought of my brothers. "What about Danny and Collin? Where are they?"

"They stayed the night with Joel," Dad said. "Charlie's gone to check on them. For the moment, you are our focus. Everything we've done for the last twelve years is a waste if something happens to you."

"Why not use technology to hide us?" I asked.

"Because technology can be defeated," Mom said. "We needed a story without questions. We needed drama with a human touch."

"Are you really from Earth?" I asked.

"Justin was born on Earth, but both of his parents were from Golvern," Mom said. "Think you had it bad? He never got to go outside when he was young. I grew up in Credence, just like I always told you. The trick about lying is it has to center around truth to be effective." She smiled. "My mother came here on an educational trip and met my father, who was human. They married, but after Charlie was born without a twin, she knew she could never go back. Even though I had Darla…" Her voice choked up.

"Aunt Charlie told me about the fire."

Mom nodded and reached for the cup of coffee. She took a long gulp.

"But didn't staying on Earth shorten her life?" I asked.

"My mother died when I was twelve," she finally said, "but we had all those wonderful years together. On Golvern, Charlie would have been sent to a separate home. She would have been tormented and never allowed to go to nursing school."

"You didn't have the sunscreen back then, did you?"

"I've been waiting for you to ask about that," Dad

said.

"They tested me last night. The doctor insisted what I wore wasn't sunscreen."

"It's a special sunscreen," Dad said. "We've worn several iterations over the years, but this version seems most effective."

"But you got sick," I said.

"So did you, with the right amount of sun. The sunscreen keeps me well for the most part, but don't forget I'm older than you. I've had many maintenance treatments over the years you never knew about. That's what we were going to Atlanta for."

"What about Mom?"

"She's half human, which has advantages."

"But your cancer, the chemo—"

"A marathon maintenance treatment, though every bit as painful as chemo, I'd imagine. The hospital in Atlanta has special doctors who know how to treat our people. That's where we took you after your sunburn."

"But that was a human hospital."

He laughed. "We call it by the name of a human hospital to stay off the radar, but I promise the hospital we were in only treats people like you and me."

His words made my skin crawl. "Why didn't Pade or Bailey notice?"

"They didn't know which questions to ask any more than you did."

"I'm sure Evelyn's doctor will figure out the secret to your sunscreen," I said. "He scraped a sample from my skin."

"Good, maybe it will help others. The discovery was made several years ago by a close friend of mine, and as much as I wanted to distribute the results beyond

Earth, it simply wasn't feasible while we were underground. Not having to die is going to be a big deal for a whole lot of people."

I watched Dad's face as he spoke, saw the hope shining in his eyes. "What happens now?"

Dad leaned his head back and closed his eyes. "We wait."

"For?" I asked.

"Whoever was trying to kill you."

CHAPTER SIXTEEN

Nowhere To Run

"We just sit and wait?"

"That's the idea," Dad said.

I couldn't believe how calm he sounded. "Aren't you going to call someone? How can you be sure it's not the Lucha Noir?"

He opened his eyes. "If the Lucha Noir were trying to kill you, I'd be the first to know."

"Are you really their leader?"

"Of course he is," Mom said. "Haven't you been listening?"

I shook my head. "For twelve years, we've moved from town to town, with barely enough money to pay the bills."

"Money was never an issue," Dad said. "But living a simple life kept us off the radar."

"What about your jobs?"

"A cover," he said. "Although Health Made Simple is a real company, dedicated to treatments which help people from Golvern live longer lives on Earth."

"Before we came to Credence, I had three outfits. Total."

Mom sighed. "I'm sorry. You deserved better, but I never realized you worried about clothes."

"I don't." I balled my fist and shook it at Dad. "You refused to let me get a license."

"You'll never need a license," Dad said. "Of that I am certain."

"A year ago, I was normal. Yesterday I was from another planet. Today I'm—"

"Important?" Dad asked.

"I'm royalty from another planet, which sounds like something you pulled from the pages of a book I've read. My brother is lying in a hospital bed, and the same people who were after him will probably come for me at any moment. And you won't call for help."

Dad's words came out in a patient flow. "I won't call because it simply isn't necessary. We mobilized a team after Lorraine found the book."

"You recognized the language," I said. "You knew the notes were written by someone from Golvern."

Dad nodded. "This hospital is surrounded by fighters with loyalty to the Lucha Noir. Dozens of fighters. If someone comes here to harm you, there'll be retribution, to say the least."

"Who's coming?" Bailey asked, with Pade following behind. She removed the cap from the bottle in her hand and took a sip.

"No one for you to worry about." Dad stood. "Wish me luck."

"Where are you going?" I asked.

"To face your mother, of course. I did make a promise."

Bailey coughed into her bottle, drizzling coke down her chin. "Mrs. Pearson is back?"

"Want me to come?" Mom asked, but the tone of her voice suggested she'd rather clean every bathroom in the hospital.

"No," Dad said, "I think just me would be better. Perhaps I can convince her not to sign our death warrants."

Bailey slumped into a chair. "Uncle Justin, please don't make jokes right now. I want to know the second you find out what's wrong with Chase."

Dad raised an eyebrow. "Hopefully Chase will be fine, but I'll add you to the list." He took another look at Mom. "Are you okay?"

"Yes." Mom looked at Pade and Bailey. "Perhaps I will check on security." She patted my hand and stood, following Dad out of the room.

Pade handed me a coke. I twisted the cap and took a sip of the fizzy liquid. It burned my throat as I dropped into one of the chairs, but it was a taste I'd miss. "I wonder if they have sodas on Golvern."

"How long have you known?" Bailey asked.

I crossed my arms. "How long have you known?"

"Since we stayed in Colorado. I lied to you about the night Dad fought with Pade. I found a way through that door."

"Mom never told us," Pade said, leaning against the window. "It feels kind of dumb knowing I've had this power for seventeen years and never knew how to use it."

"Your turn," Bailey said.

"I dreamed about Chase the night you and Pade left for Colorado. I remembered running away, and that

Chase was my brother, but nothing before. My power didn't return until after the coma."

"Mom said you got a reboot," Bailey said. She shrugged as Pade gave her the 'can't believe you said that' look. "I wanted you to tell me, but I couldn't wait. I had to know."

"How long have you known about me?" I asked.

"Since the car, when Chase said you were his sister. Do you remember everything now?"

"No," I said. "Chase took me to the spaceship last night, but my real mother doesn't even know how to help."

"You went up there?" Bailey asked, pointing at the ceiling.

"Would you have gone back to Golvern without saying goodbye?" Pade asked, his words almost a whisper.

I looked into his eyes, unsure of how to answer. "I didn't."

"That's not what I asked."

"Imagine what it would be like on Golvern," Bailey said as her eyes grew with wonder. "Mom told us about the two suns and all of the water."

Pade snickered. "I'd never go there. We'd be outcasts, remember? They don't want people there who don't have a twin."

Bailey stared at me. "Chase once told me his birthday was October fourteenth. Is that your birthday too?"

"Yes," I said.

"That means you'll be seventeen before me. Why didn't you tell me?"

"I didn't think you'd understand."

"*We* didn't think *you'd* understand about *our* power. If only we'd talked before. This whole situation makes me mad." Bailey's face lit up and she snapped her fingers. "Let's play truth or dare, but without the dare part."

"That's just truth," Pade said.

"Right," Bailey said, "that's what we need more of around here."

I thought of the night at Angel's house. "Did you really spill the tequila?"

Bailey giggled. "Guilty. And the Ouija board—that was me too. What about those Ronald rumors?"

"That he's crazy?" I smiled. "I might have had something to do with that."

Pade frowned and took a sip of his coke. "Football."

"What?" I asked, choking on my drink.

"Prepare yourself," Bailey said.

Pade laughed, his face twisting in misery. "Why do you think people always said I had a gift for throwing a football? Turns out I was using my power and didn't know it."

I smiled, wishing I was close enough to touch him. "You should have told me."

"I wanted to tell you so many times." Pade crossed the floor to stand before me. "Then I learned about New York and realized you really were different. I knew I needed to find the right way to tell you, otherwise you'd never understand. I considered showing you my power, but I was afraid of scaring you."

"If only you had."

"That day when Collin got hurt, when you opened your eyes and looked up at me, I almost spilled everything. I never wanted to lie to you, but Mom insisted." He shook his head, disgust souring his features. "She knew you were like us all along. I can't believe she made me lie."

"Do you forgive me for wanting to go back?" I asked.

He cleared his throat. "Now that the secrets are out, be honest. How do you really feel about me?"

I pulled the gold chain from under my shirt.

He stared, a glistening ray of hope spreading across his face, as if I'd said three words instead.

* * * * *

"The boys are fine," Aunt Charlie said to Mom, as I reached Chase's room. "Not a single car has passed down our street that doesn't belong, but I don't know how long before someone realizes we're in this hospital. It could be worse if—"

"Jes," Mom said. "You can see Chase now."

I looked from Mom to Aunt Charlie. Both stared at me with pity, but their eyes also held a love that was undeniable. I couldn't find an ounce of hatred within me for either of them.

Evelyn sat next to the bed where an IV tube ran into Chase's arm. The machine next to him beeped and groaned, giving a series of vitals that seemed almost normal. Maybe I was wrong to worry. She held his hand, whispered his name, and touched his hair with the other hand. Dad stood near the tiny window, staring as I approached the bed. Evelyn looked up, shifting to stand, but I waved her to stay in the chair. Circling the bed, I gripped Chase's other hand.

I stood and listened as Chase's chest rose and fell. His eyelids fluttered, but never opened. Evelyn hummed a soft tune, one that made me feel cozy inside. As if I was never lost on another planet a million miles away. Like I could take on the world and win. Her eyes met mine with a softness and understanding so real I couldn't look away. She held out an arm and I moved to her side of the bed. Her hand brought a warmth to my cheek that dissolved the uncertainty in my stomach.

Dad checked a message on his phone and approached the bed. "There's more to this story Jes... Kayden," he said, correcting himself as Evelyn frowned. "Whatever Chase joined wasn't the Lucha Noir."

"There is another opposition group?" Her eyes grew wide.

"If Chase were with the Lucha Noir, I'd know. My guess is he's in danger, but not from the Lucha Noir. You've got to get him back to Golvern."

"And my daughter?"

Looking away, Dad sighed. "You can't protect them both. I think we've proven that."

Evelyn took my hand, squeezing as she let out a sob. Her eyes held a longing, deep enough for an ocean of tears. "We are out of time."

"Wait," I said, as the truth dawned. "You're leaving me with them?"

She gripped my hand as if she'd never let go. "If what your... *dad* says is correct, Chase is in more trouble than I imagined. He trusted the wrong people and has managed to lead them to you. I am sorry, but to keep you safe, we must keep the two of you apart."

No matter what happened, I had to lose someone. I felt like crying again, at the unfairness of it all, but my eyes stayed dry. Evelyn couldn't hide her fear for Chase or her fear for me. She was willing to trust the people who raised me. No one had a choice.

"I wish things were different this time," she said. "My darling, I cannot imagine another day without you."

A gun appeared in Dad's hand. "How many guards did you bring?"

"Two outside the doors," she said. "Another six outside the hospital. Please do not harm them."

"We will try to escape without casualties, but it's important they think we're stealing Kayden away."

"Why does it matter?" I asked.

"Because," Dad said, "we don't know who Chase is involved with. It could be one or more of her guards. We will give your mother a diversion to get Chase out of here safely."

She nodded. "The Lucha Noir will protect my daughter?"

"Until our deaths. She is the Honra Ril," he said, pushing me forward. "Our Honored Girl. Say your goodbyes but know you will see them again. I promise."

I hugged my mother and leaned over Chase, kissing his cheek. "And I promise *you* I'll come back."

"We'll buy you ten minutes to get him unhooked and back to your ship," Dad said. He pulled me out of the room and into the crowded hall. Mom rushed forward, from where she stood by the door.

"Update?" Dad asked.

"Charlie took Pade and Bailey back to the house. They'll drive to Joel's and have the boys back in ten. Two guards outside the doors and another six outside the building."

"Good, she was honest with us." Dad looked at

Mom as he led us to the exit. "Signal our fighters to stand down. It's important the guards think we're taking her by force."

Force? "What do you mean—"

"Scream when appropriate," Mom said.

As the doors opened, a blast of voices hit us. We shuffled through the main E.R. waiting room, squeezing between two wheelchairs and a man with crutches. The man was waving one in the air, complaining about the wait.

"Gun!" a nurse on the other side of the reception window screamed.

Dad gripped my arm as two men in black suits rushed forward. "Get down," he yelled as if commanding an army of troops. Waving the gun brought more screams from around the room. The man with crutches stumbled into a nearby observation room. People around us ran for the sliding doors, fighting to escape into the night.

Dad fired the gun, hitting a bullseye with the three cameras, each at a different corner of the room. Shards of glass rained down on the remaining people.

"What are you doing?" I asked.

"Saw that on TV," he said. "Always wanted to try it."

One of the guards reached for me. Mom punched him in the stomach and hooked her foot behind his knee. The man fell to the ground as she kicked his side.

Dad shoved his elbow into the other guard's face. The man groaned, grabbing for his face as Dad hurled him over a row of chairs. "Two down."

Mom took a gun from the hand of the man under her foot. She looked over it, scrunching her nose.

"These weapons used to have a paralyzer setting."

"Here," Dad said and reached for the gun, "let me help."

"No," she said, "it hasn't been that long. Let me figure it out."

Dad laughed. "Don't kill anyone while you're figuring it out."

She hit a button and fired at a nearby trash can. The plastic disintegrated, leaving nothing but a square burn on the floor. "That wasn't it. How much longer?"

He looked at his watch. "We need to give them at least five more minutes."

Mom hit another button and fired the gun, this time at an empty wheelchair. The metal glowed, but when the light faded, the chair remained. She smiled, satisfied with herself.

"Come on." Dad pulled me toward the sliding doors. He circled an arm around my waist, lifting me over his shoulder.

"Now," Mom said.

I screamed and kicked my feet, fighting against Dad as he carried me outside, but I couldn't see the people running around us, not with my perfect view of the ground. Crashes sounded from where row after row of cars were parked, along with spinning tires as people raced to exit the parking lot. He turned around and around, until I felt like puking.

"Surely, they've seen us," Mom said.

"Why don't we just zap ourselves home?" I asked as he sat me down on my feet.

A popping noise sounded as something hit the ground near my feet.

Mom shot at a man in a suit and he fell to the

ground, frozen in place. Another guard appeared and Mom spun around, hitting him with a second shot.

A high-pitched sound zipped by my head.

"For goodness sake Jes," Mom said, "get down."

"Down where?"

"Anywhere," they both said at the same time.

"I'll cover her." Mom waved me behind her. We ran along the row of shrubs and dove between two cars.

Dad fired a series of shots and ran through the shrubs, sliding on the gravel around the square bushes as he reached the pavement. He landed next to us, almost on his knees.

"A little out of shape?" Mom asked.

"I don't know if I'll make it to Atlanta at this rate." He coughed, a ragged sound I feared worse than any gun.

"You weren't making up being sick," I said.

He put an arm around me. "Sorry for all of this. The timing couldn't have been worse. If we make it out alive, I promise to teach you how to drive."

I couldn't help but laugh, sitting next to my parents, wedged between two cars because armed guards from another planet were shooting at us.

Dad checked his watch again. "Want to do the honors?" he asked Mom.

"I can get myself home," I said.

He grinned, pride shining in his eyes. "That's my girl."

CHAPTER SEVENTEEN

One More Goodbye

When we appeared in the empty living room, Mom and Dad both stared at me, a look of awe on their faces.

"You said you'd get yourself home," Dad said, "but I wasn't sure. I heard the fear in your voice."

"Yeah, I was scared. People were shooting at us."

"Fear is an issue," Mom said. "It's the biggest obstacle to using our power. Most people spend years mastering that skill. Adult years. Some never do."

"But you figured it out," Dad said. "In two months, you've found a way to tap into your power. Then you set aside fear when you needed your power the most."

"It's no big deal," I said.

Mom looked incredulous. "It's a *huge* deal."

Voices sounded as Danny and Collin opened the front door, protesting before Dad could say the word 'move.'

Dad held up his hands. "No arguing. You know how this works. You've got twenty minutes. Pack whatever will fit in your bags."

He looked at me. "Only take what's most important to you. Everything else we'll buy along the way."

"You don't care about us," Danny whined. "You only care about Jes. Everything we do is for her."

"You're right." Dad looked at his watch. "You're pushing nineteen. Want to complain some more?"

"Don't argue with your father," Mom said, with a frigid strictness I never knew she had.

Danny's mouth fell open.

"We want to stay in Credence," Collin yelled over and over, as they climbed the stairs.

"Don't tell them anything about tonight," Mom said. "It's safer that way."

"Do they know about our power?" I asked.

Mom laughed. "Thank goodness, no. We might never get them in the car."

"I fear they're getting close to figuring it out," Dad said, "and I can only imagine the drama when they do."

"I still can't believe you hid the truth all these years."

He grinned. "It wasn't so hard, but it did get strange the day Collin was hurt. When Pade called, I was still ten minutes from the house. I pulled my truck over and came immediately. Bailey had brought Danny inside to clean up. Collin was out cold. I thought he'd *lost* too much blood and took him to the hospital, but it turns out his issue is with *seeing* too much blood. Lorraine circled back in the van to grab Danny."

"Danny talked through what happened," Mom said. "All the way to the hospital. I'm not sure if the sight of you or Collin scared him worse."

"When you freaked out," Dad said, "I wasn't sure how to handle you, save Collin, and keep our secret at the same time."

"Good thing Pade was there," Mom said, giving me a wink.

Dad didn't notice as he checked his watch. "Sixteen. Clock is ticking, Jes."

"What about Bailey and Pade? What's going to happen with them?"

Mom started for her bedroom. "They can't go where we're going."

I shivered at the finality in her voice. "Where is that?"

"You'll find out when we get there," Dad said, looking down at me. "You'll have to trust us, but I will tell you this is going to be an all-nighter."

"Can I say goodbye?"

Mom stopped in the doorway and she and Dad exchanged a look. She nodded and typed a message into her phone. In a matter of seconds, Aunt Charlie appeared in the living room, with Bailey and Pade not far away.

Bailey put her arms around my neck. "Was Chase okay?" she whispered.

"Yes," I whispered, forcing what confidence I could find into my voice, though I wasn't sure. "He's going home."

She nodded and wiped a palm across her eyes. "Are those people still after him?"

"I don't think so." Another lie, but my words had the effect of calming the fear in her voice.

Bailey pulled away. "I'll miss you."

Pade stepped up, hugging me as if we hardly knew each other. Then he moved away, his eyes revealing nothing about the way he felt. "See you, short… stuff."

So, we were back to the ban on cuss words? I smiled. "I'll miss you too."

He nodded and turned away as Aunt Charlie hugged me and then reached for her sister. Mom and Aunt Charlie held each other as if they might not meet again for years. I couldn't take my eyes off them as they cried. Even Dad seemed hesitant to break up their goodbye.

When they finally disappeared, I climbed the stairs. Time for the dreaded task of getting ready to move again. I'd only been here thirty times before. What was once more?

From under my bed, I pulled the striped bag and the roller with stars, preparing to fill them as I had on the night we'd come to Credence. I looked over my dresser, selecting a few of my favorite memorabilia accrued over the years. Racing through my closet at ninety-miles an hour, I grabbed my best fitting jeans and a couple of shirts.

I noticed the sweater and hat I'd worn the night before, in a crumpled pile near the bed. I grabbed them and tossed them in the bag. As for everything else—I didn't need it anymore. No reason for more reminders that my whole life had been a lie.

On my dresser sat the book. I lifted the copy of *Pride and Prejudice* my mother gave me, gripping it to my chest. It was her favorite. No way could I leave it behind this time. I placed the book in my bag, safely between my clothes, and zipped the bag. As I turned to survey the room one last time, I jumped when I heard a sound behind me.

"Hey," Pade whispered.

I threw my arms around him. He took my hand and wrapped his fingers over mine, but when he released my hand I felt something cold against my skin—a slim golden ring, accented by a row of tiny diamonds around its center. Turning the ring over and over in my hand, I looked into his eyes. "Skip gave Angel a promise ring."

"This isn't a promise ring," he said gruffly. "This is a 'I plan to marry you' ring. It belonged to my grandfather. He gave this ring to my grandmother when she moved to Earth."

"Mom's parents?"

He nodded. "I'd get down on one knee but there isn't time. We're going back to Colorado."

"You still want to be with me?" I asked, pulling his face to mine. I thought the longing welling inside would tear me apart. "You wanted to at Terrance's house."

He smiled with a glint of humor. "I'd be lying if I said I don't, but we've got to hurry. Your parents will be ready to leave at any moment."

"But when?"

"Wait for me," he said softly. "Wherever you go, I'll find you." Pade circled his arms around me and pulled me against his chest. "No matter how long it takes, I will find you. I promise."

Our lips were barely an inch apart. He released a breath and I inhaled. Pulling me even closer, I exhaled as he drew a breath. I closed my eyes as happiness surged through my veins. Every inch of my skin longed for the feel of his hands.

"You feel it too?" he whispered.

"Yes," I said, struggling to form the words. I didn't want to talk, I simply wanted to live in this feeling forever.

He ran a thumb over my lips. "Then you finally understand."

"Understand what?" The only thing I understood was how I might melt under his gaze.

"How I felt the first day we kissed."

I opened my eyes. Already the corners were stinging with a salty moisture I must hold back.

"Don't cry," Pade said. "Your dad is on the stairs. Can't you hear him?"

All I could hear was my own heartbeat thudding in my ears. "I'll wait."

"Good," he said and kissed me.

My heart hammered faster, though this wasn't like our kiss on the trestle. This was goodbye. I closed my eyes again, this time wrapped in a beautiful bliss, wishing the kiss would never end.

"I love you," I whispered when his lips left mine.

The door to my bedroom flew open.

"It's time," Dad said.

I opened my eyes. Pade was gone.

"Grab your bags, Jes. No need to cry over this place. You never know, we might make it back here someday. But right now, we've got to go."

I closed my hand over the ring.

* * * * *

With a bag in each hand, I walked through our front door for the last time. *It's just another move*, I told myself, like all the others we'd made over the last twelve years.

Mom stood in the driveway, loading bags into the back of a black car.

"Get in," she said.

I looked from her to the van, sitting lonely next to this new car.

She noticed my hesitation. "We won't be driving the van anymore. Too many people know our patterns."

Nodding, I placed the roller suitcase in the trunk of the car.

"There won't be room for both bags," she said. "You'll have to hold one at your feet for now." She looked over me, then touched the side of my face. "I'm sorry you've had to live like this, Kayden. We wanted to protect you, not take the life of luxury that should have been yours away."

"I'll forgive you, but only on one condition."

"Which is?" she asked.

"Call me Jes."

She pulled me into her arms. "You never cease to amaze me."

I climbed into the backseat, thankful I'd beat the boys. One of them would have to sit in the middle. The striped bag and my purse fit at my feet, leaving more than enough room to stretch out. The seat under me felt softer than the couch I'd always slept on in the house near Phoenix. I leaned my head back, inhaling the new car smell. In twelve years, we'd never had a new car.

The boys, still whining about having to leave, argued about who would sit in the middle. It wasn't a big deal—four of us could have ridden comfortably in that seat. Still, I kept my mouth shut as I pulled my MP3 player from the bag. Digging through the bag, I made sure the book was there while I still had light.

Dad opened the door in front of me and climbed into the driver's seat. "It's been awhile since I sat so low."

Mom got in the passenger seat and closed her door. "It feels like we're sitting on the ground."

He looked in the mirror. "Okay back there?"

Danny and Collin said "no," with perfect timing as always. I smiled in the darkness as my pillow appeared in my lap. The boys were too busy sulking to notice.

"Get some sleep," Dad said, backing the car out of the driveway.

Beyond the dark glass, I watched Pade's window for any sign of movement. As the car pulled onto the road, I thought I saw a shift in the blinds, no more than a sliver of a gap between the manila strips.

Then we were out of the neighborhood, heading for the interstate.

I patted the necklace under my shirt and traced the ring with a flutter of my heart. Without the moon to guide us, the sky felt like a nightmare called from along the horizon.

Was Chase and my mother on a ship somewhere above us or had they managed to find their way back to Golvern? I had a feeling many nightmares would come and go before I'd see them again.

I'd probably never see Rachelle or Angel again. Angel and Skip would have their happy ending, I was sure. But I wanted to see Rachelle, to tell her I didn't hate her. Losing these friends brought a fresh round of tears to my eyes. How could I possibly have more? I pushed the thought away. No more tears after tonight.

Would I see Pade and Bailey again? He'd promised to find me, but how could he when *I* didn't even know which planet I'd be on tomorrow?

The car merged onto an empty highway. Only lights from two eighteen wheelers could be seen in the distance. I read another sign for Credence as we passed the last exit for miles. With the hum of tires, I closed my eyes and faded off to sleep.

PADE

He watched as she climbed into the back of a black Lexus. It was a fast car. No doubt it was one they could disappear in.

"I miss her already," Bailey said. She split the blinds wider, but the room was dark enough no one would notice. "You think Dad bought their car?"

"Probably." Their dad had bought everything else.

"Did you tell her how you feel?"

His sister had always insisted he belonged with Jes. Although he usually hated to admit she was right, this time he didn't mind. "I asked her to wait for me. I gave her the ring." And she'd finally said the words that wiped every question from his mind.

A smile spread across her face, one with more sadness than she deserved. "Jes will understand. I only wish Granddaddy were here. He wanted the ring to go to someone special."

He laughed bitterly. "I kept my promise. No one's more special than Jes."

"Yeah," Bailey said. "I wonder if they'll visit us in Colorado."

The car sped away, tail lights fading over the last hill and into the darkness. "I get the feeling they won't be visiting anyone."

The light above them burst to life. "Ready?" their mother asked. Her arms were crossed where she leaned against the door frame.

Bailey swung around. "We're leaving for Dad's place tonight?"

The woman's eyes were tired. "There's no telling who will show up next door. They'll ransack the house when they realize it's empty, maybe even burn it down. I can't go through that."

"Where did they go?" he asked.

"I honestly don't know," she said. "Lorraine doesn't even know yet. It's safer that way."

"How will you find them again?"

She looked him over before answering. "Lorraine and I have lived through our own share of rough times, long before you were born. We've been separated by a sea of stars, but we've always managed to find each other."

"How much time do we have?" Bailey started for the door. "I've got to get my clothes and my makeup. I can't walk through the airport with my eyeliner looking like I've been standing on a street corner."

Her mother frowned. "You won't need any clothes. Or makeup for that matter. You'll have everything you need when we arrive."

Something was wrong. "We're driving to Colorado?" he asked.

"No one's going to Colorado," she said. "As of now, I won't insist we do things the human way anymore."

Bailey grabbed her mother's arm. "You said we were moving to Dad's."

"We're moving to your father's house on Golvern."

Acknowledgements

I want to thank you for reading this book. Please consider leaving an honest review.

Thanks to:

Tommy for reading this story before it was complete. I appreciate his insights, his candor, and the fact that he's a nice guy (though I promised I'd never admit this to anyone).

Jodi for reading this story and for reminding me what I love most about young adult books.

Carla for reading *Leftover Girl* while it was a mess and still talking to me afterward.

Becky for being my eleventh-hour beta reader.

Christie at EbookEditingPro. Her suggestions were spot-on and forced me to dig deeper. The results made me enjoy the story even more. I'd be thrilled for her to hand me a shovel any day.

Tabitha at Tacal Designs for the beautiful cover design. I knew when I saw it, that was Jes.

Carole P. Roman for all of her insights into publishing. Not only does she write books and blog, she helped this indie writer navigate the uncharted waters. I could never thank her enough for reaching out.

My husband, for without his help none of this would be possible. He understands and encourages me even on the days when I wonder how he can.

About The Author

C.C. Bolick grew up in south Alabama, where she's happy to still reside. She's an engineer by day and a writer by night—too bad she could never do one without the other.

Please visit her website at www.ccbolick.com for updates on future releases.

Made in the USA
Coppell, TX
19 July 2020